SHADOW CRIMES

E. J. MORAN

ISBN: 0999523503
ISBN 13: 9780999523506
Library of Congress Control Number: 2017915911
Tree Lane Press, Oak Forest, IL

Dedicated to all those who suffer in silence at the hands of those who abuse their power.

Contents

PROLOGUE

Port Chester, New York, July 4ᵀᴴ, 1967

Seven-year-old Anna awoke to her grumbling stomach and the wafting scent of the pancakes her mother was making. As she enjoyed the delicious aroma, she thought about the exciting parade they were going to later that day. Anna's father, Patrick, didn't have to work at the factory, nor her mother, Gina, at Anna's grandparents' summer produce stand. It was July 4th and everyone took the day off to celebrate. Everyone, rich or poor.

Reliving vivid memories from the year before, Anna recalled how her father hoisted her up onto his shoulders so she could see far above the crowds. Mesmerized by the floats soaring past, the glittery costumed young girls throwing batons into the air, and the young boys playing instruments as they marched ahead of the city's uniformed policemen, she sat entranced until she spotted her uncle, a young recruit with the New York Police Department. Bubbling over with excitement, she waved her little American flag with joy and cheered loudly as he looked straight at her, giving her a special salute. She felt so proud at that moment, and so very loved.

Gina, originally from Sicily, called out in Italian for her daughter to come to her. "Anna, vieni qui."

Anna sprang out of bed and ran into the kitchen, eager to help her mother cook.

"Your turn, tesoro," her mother said. She handed Anna, her little treasure, a bowl of soupy, raw ingredients.

Anna grabbed the bowl and scooped up a spoon of the liquid, plopping it on the griddle.

"Wow," she exclaimed as the griddle seared with a sizzle.

"Paddy," Gina called out to her Irish-American husband when breakfast was ready.

Making his way into the kitchen, Patrick sat down at the worn-out wooden table. Gina served up the pancakes, slathering them with butter and maple syrup.

"Looks yummy," he said.

Anna perched herself on a chair and began devouring her breakfast.

"Don't eat so quickly, Anna, you'll choke. You won't enjoy any of it either," her father said in a sharp tone.

"Yes, Papa," Anna replied softly, fearful of her father's unpredictable moods.

Smiling at her, he continued to savor the sweet flavor of the pancakes, making a point of eating each bite slowly. Anna relaxed—it was still going to be a good day. Just like last year, her father was in a good mood on this 4th of July.

"OK, Anna, help your mother clean the kitchen so we can get the show on the road."

Jumping up from her chair, Anna sprang into action. "What time do we leave, Papa?"

The parade was taking place on North Main Street this year and Anna's father wanted to make sure they got a good view.

"Soon, sweetheart. Mama is seven months pregnant, and we need to walk because our car isn't working."

Anna knew this was not entirely true. Her mother had a big stomach, so she was definitely pregnant, but Anna thought the car worked fine. She had heard her Uncle Mickey, the police officer, telling her father that he couldn't drive anymore. Anna wasn't quite sure why, but whatever her father said was never to be argued with.

"I'm going to take a bath," he said, leaving his wife and daughter to clean up.

Anna turned her attention back to her mother. "Mama, how come you never drive?"

"Tesoro, I don't have a license," Gina said as she gathered up the plates and cutlery from the table and took them over to the sink.

"What's a license?"

"It's like a permission slip to drive."

"Oh." Anna was still confused.

"Never mind dear." Gina handed Anna a wet cloth. "Wash off the table please."

Anna eagerly began wiping the table clean. "How long will it take us to get the parade?"

"Not too long, tesoro, about thirty minutes. I may have to rest a bit along the way because I'm carrying your new brother or sister, so we'll take our time."

"Yes, Mama, you need to be careful," Anna said, handing the dishcloth back to her mother.

"I know, tesoro, don't worry." Gina embraced Anna, kissing her affectionately on the head. Then she looked out the kitchen window and prayed. "Oh Dio, I hope the weather stays nice for the parade. The weatherman said a storm was brewing."

When they left the house, the weather was still glorious and the birds were singing. Once they reached North Main Street, the same road Gina took to her parents' produce stand, they were confronted with an onslaught of traffic because the street still hadn't been cordoned off for the parade. Suddenly a crackle of lightning lit the air, followed by a huge rumble and a torrent of rain.

"Walk single file," Anna's father shouted through the downpour. "Anna, right behind me," he said, deciding Anna would be safest sandwiched in-between him and his wife.

"I can't see," her mother yelled.

Trucks were splashing through puddles and kicking up the rain, blinding all three of them as they walked along the road. Suddenly, Anna heard a loud bang and her mother let out a terrifying scream. A truck skidded past them through the muddy puddles and abruptly came to a halt. Anna didn't understand what was going on. She felt like she was in a dream; everything seemed to be happening in slow motion. She saw her mother sprawled out on the side of the road crying in agony and her father running through the rain toward her mother. Confused, she stared in disbelief as the deluge of torrential rain finally turned to a drizzle. Through watery eyes she saw an image that would stay with her forever—her mother on the side of the road, bloodied and moaning. Anna ran to her parents. Her father was slumped over, sobbing over her mother's bloody, half-conscious body.

"Mama!" Anna screamed.

Gina looked weakly at Anna and, through heavy breaths, uttered her last words. "I love you, tesoro. Take care of our family."

She fell unconscious and Patrick let out an anguished wail. Dazed, Anna stared ahead while tears trickled down her cheeks.

Cars and trucks began backing up, sirens started sounding, and soon the town's only ambulance arrived. Three emergency service responders—medics recently back from the Vietnam War—jumped out and sprang into action. Gingerly, they put Gina on a gurney and ushered Patrick and Anna into the ambulance. Patrick was distraught and Anna couldn't grasp what was happening. The medics hooked Gina up to a resuscitator and feverishly tried to save her life while the ambulance sped to the hospital.

The medics knew Anna's unconscious mother was near death due to internal bleeding when blood trickled out from the side of her mouth. It would be a matter of minutes before her heart stopped.

"We need to save the baby!" a medic shouted.

The ambulance screeched to a halt in front of the emergency entrance to the hospital. The medics jumped out, sliding out the gurney that held Gina. She was rushed into the hospital as Patrick and Anna followed closely behind.

"Wait there," one of the medics said, motioning toward the waiting room.

Grief-stricken, Patrick was shaking and sobbing at the thought of losing his beloved wife and new baby. Anna was in a complete state of shock; it was too much for a seven-year-old to comprehend.

The medics rushed Gina through the double doors, shouting for a doctor. One came quickly, and after one of the medics explained the urgency of the situation the doctor prepared himself and Gina for emergency surgery while nurses clamored to the scene and began scrambling for instruments. The doctor made a long incision across Gina's still abdomen, releasing a torrent of blood. Finally, the team managed to stop the bleeding and a tiny wailing cry was heard.

A baby boy was born.

NEW YORK 1978

CHAPTER 1

APRIL NIGHT

The buzz of the intercom surprised Rhonda. It was 11:00 p.m. and she was about to go to sleep.

"Hello?" she said.

"Hello, Rhonda?"

The man identified himself and she recognized his name immediately. "What are you doing here?"

"Sorry. I know it's late. I wanted to speak to you earlier but couldn't because there were too many other models around. I may have a potential opportunity just for you."

"Oh?" She was dead tired and the last thing she wanted was unexpected company. Nevertheless, she didn't feel she could say no to any possible break that presented itself. She was desperate to make it in the modeling world.

"OK. Let me buzz you up." She opened the front door and waited for the rickety vintage elevator at the far end of the hall to set in motion. It was completely black, so she turned on the hall lights. She thought about how crazy she had been to rent an apartment in a building that was mostly for commercial use. The building was totally empty at night, as was the surrounding area. It was the meatpacking district after all. No one ever showed up until around 6:00 a.m. Yes, the rent was dirt cheap, but in hindsight it was a huge mistake. How could she know any better though? She was only eighteen—a complete babe in the woods. Not only that, no one had taught her *anything*. Growing up, her mom worked every day, and most nights, to support her and her younger sisters. Her father was nowhere in sight, never had been. So with no money and no father she knew very little about how to make decisions; she just had pure ambition. That's what lead her to NYC, hardly a penny in her pocket, to become a model.

The clattering elevator came to a halt. Its passenger opened the scissor gate, then the double door, and exited. "Thank you for letting me up," he said as he walked toward Rhonda.

"Hi," she said sweetly. "Come on in." Rhonda motioned him through the door. "I'm really sorry but I'm already in my nightgown. I was about to go to sleep."

"Of course, it's late." He glanced around the miniscule studio. It was neat and barren, apart from a tiny, decrepit kitchenette, a single bed, and a small side table lined with a few of Rhonda's modeling photos. "So, this is the apartment you were talking about?" he said, shaking his head in dismay. "You can do better than this. It's horrible here."

"It is, isn't it?" Rhonda said, putting her head down with embarrassment. "Unfortunately though, I couldn't afford more." Regaining her composure, she smiled softly. "Anyway, the good news is I pay month-to-month, and as soon as I make some decent money modeling I'm going to move out."

"That's what I wanted to speak to you about."

"Well, have a seat," she said, laughing as she motioned to a corner at the far end of the bed. "Can I get you something to drink first?" she asked as he sat down.

"No, nothing, thank you." He looked at her intently, following her every gesture as she perched herself down near the head of the bed.

"So, you want to be a famous model?"

She nodded in agreement.

"Let's talk about what I can do for you."

"Terrific," she said, overjoyed by his interest in helping her.

"I think you have a lot of potential. I really do."

Rhonda smiled eagerly and took in a big breath of air, emphasizing her svelte, perfect figure.

"It's not easy though to make it as a model. Beautiful girls are a dime a dozen," he said.

"I know. It's true. I see so many beautiful models every day."

"Exactly. That's why you need someone with connections, someone with power, to help you."

"You're right," Rhonda said. She could hardly believe she may be about to get her lucky break, one that could launch her to stardom in the modeling world.

Suddenly, he reached for her arm and pulled her toward him.

"Hey, what are you doing?" Rhonda's eager smile faded. Confused, she tried to pull away.

"You know what I'm doing, Rhonda."

"No I don't. You said you wanted to speak with me."

"You want help? You want to make it big?"

"Yes, but not this way." She struggled to get away, but her resistance made him angry.

"You know you want this. I could see it in your eyes earlier."

"No I don't," she said, still trying to pull away as his fingers dug into her arms.

He didn't loosen his grip. "You are so sexy, don't you know that?"

"Stop. I don't want to do this. I'm still a virgin."

"A virgin?" He pushed her back and held on to her tightly with outstretched arms, his piercing stare locking onto her terrified eyes. "I don't believe you."

"I am, I swear!" She tried to loosen his grip and get up from the bed. "You got the wrong impression."

"Then why are you such a cockteaser?" His large almond-shaped eyes began to shrink as he held her firmly and squinted at her with the most evil look she had ever seen.

"I'm not. I don't know what you're talking about."

Pulling her closer, he kissed her hard as she desperately made futile attempts to get away.

"You slut!"

Rhonda squirmed and dodged his attempts to kiss her, shrieking in terror. He wrestled her down on the bed, straddling her hips and pushing her down against the pillow. He smothered her face with one of his large hands, both to shut her up and hold her still. Terrified, she froze.

"Cockteaser! You're like all the others," he hissed.

Using his free hand, he undid his trousers and forced himself inside her. Rhonda could only whimper, too paralyzed with fear to do anything else. He grew more and more excited with each thrust, mumbling incoherent words of disgust and hatred until he reached his climax.

Rhonda bled to death in her own bed, her throat sliced with a seven-inch combat knife.

⋏

"Looks like she's been dead a few days," Detective Tansey said as he stared at Rhonda's decomposing body. The ruggedly handsome man held his cool demeanor while the two officers from the crime lab covered their noses—the room was beginning to have a foul smell.

"Do you think she was a model?" Officer Kasinski asked.

"Maybe." Tansey glanced over at the professional-looking photos of Rhonda on the nightstand. "Definitely not a famous one though if she was living in a place like this."

"Unless she was a druggie. Could have spent all her money on cocaine or something," Officer Smith added.

"True, seen that before," Tansey said.

Kasinski checked out the bathroom and returned. "No signs of drug paraphernalia."

Tansey searched Rhonda's outstretched arms. "No signs of track marks either. She must have been living in this shithole because it was cheap."

The men shook their heads in disgust at the level of violence.

"Killer didn't just cut her throat, he damn near took her head off," Smith said.

"Looks like she's been raped too, judging by the bruising," Tansey added.

"My guess is that she let him up here," Kasinski continued. "The intercom works, and there are no apparent signs of forced entry. That is, unless he was already in the building and snuck into her apartment while she slept. The lock is a joke."

"Or maybe she brought him home with her," Smith countered.

"Possibly. OK, let's get to work. We don't need to stare at her anymore." Tansey glanced away from the dead girl and began assessing the room for more evidence.

A few hours later, he picked up Rhonda's telephone and called the coroner's office. The men had collected everything that could be useful; now it was time to have the poor girl removed from the putrid, blood-soaked bed and taken to the morgue.

CHAPTER 2

July Discovery

"Joey, vieni qui," Maria Gallo said, instructing her young grandson to come closer to their produce stand alongside a backcountry road in Greenwich, Connecticut.

"Why can't I play in the woods? It's boring here. There's nothing to do," Joey said, kicking up dirt as he pouted and walked back toward his grandmother. She gave him a stern look, daring him to move away. Defeated, he picked up an apple and placed it on his head. "Watch, Anna, look what I can do," he said as he tried to walk while balancing the apple.

"Wow, you're pretty good at that," Anna said, glancing over at her rambunctious eleven-year-old brother and smiling affectionately.

Joey grinned and continued clumsily attempting to balance the apple on his head. Even though he was hindered by thick glasses that barely corrected his vision, he was in constant motion—exploring, playing and getting into trouble. Anna was devoted to him, determined to better his life and keep him under her wing. She turned back and continued helping her grandmother lay out the day's stock of fruit and vegetables.

A few feet away, their grandfather, Carmelo, lifted a barrel of fruit from the bed of a rickety red pickup and started walking toward the produce stand. "We have busy day ahead. It's July 4th weekend and everyone coming here from New York City to celebrate," he said in broken English to no one in particular.

A terrible sinking feeling overcame Anna and landed in the pit of her stomach. For her, July 4th would forever be remembered as the day her pregnant mother was killed by a truck while she and her family walked to see a parade. She was so young when it happened, only seven, and much of what followed was still a blur. However, memories of her little brother, born prematurely on the day of her mother's death, were as vivid as her mother's final words instructing her to take care of the family.

Joey was a miracle baby, but laden with health issues from the start. Anna remembered visiting him at the hospital. He was so cute, with a sprout of black curly hair already covering his tiny head. Unlike Anna, who had bright red hair and green eyes like her Irish-American father, Joey resembled her beloved mother. Everyone in the family adored him and showered little Joey with love and affection. But the similarity between her little brother's looks and her deceased mother stirred up heavy emotions in Anna, leaving her with memories that were bittersweet.

Emotionally ill-equipped to deal with a premature infant son and the death of his wife, her father began drinking more. His temper became fierce and his behavior erratic. Soon he was drunk most days, leaving the responsibility of looking after a newborn and a little girl in the hands of his in-laws, Maria and Carmelo Gallo. Less than two years later he dropped dead from a heart attack, but not before leaving nine-year-old Anna emotionally scarred.

"Joey, take apple off your head. First customer of day is here," Carmelo said, noticing an intimidating shinny blue stretch limousine pull up in the dirt driveway next to the produce stand.

The Gallos and their grandchildren stared curiously. These were certainly important people, as were many in the town of Greenwich. The driver, sporting dark sunglasses, a well-tailored blue suit and a shiny cap, stepped out and opened the back door. A tall, thin, fashionably dressed woman with large black sunglasses emerged.

"I'd like to buy a dozen of these peaches please," the lady said, her voice both cheerful and slightly haughty.

"Of course," Anna replied as she busied herself gathering perfect peaches for this intriguing customer, unaware of the elegant woman's intense gaze. "Will that be all?"

"Yes, for today." The woman smiled warmly.

Her driver took her purchase and paid the bill, allowing the mysterious woman to inconspicuously check Anna's physique from head to toe. Unbeknownst to Anna, she was serving Natasha Burns, owner of Top Form Management, the most famous modeling agency in New York City.

Slipping back into the car, Natasha rolled up the partition separating her from the driver, Sergio, and turned to her companion. "Did you see that extraordinary beauty, Jo Ellen?"

"I did. She's drop-dead gorgeous," Jo Ellen said.

"That red hair is to die for. And those green eyes … they're mesmerizing," Natasha continued.

Jo Ellen, a booker at Top Form as well as Natasha's cousin, saw where this was going and egged Natasha on. "And those legs, they never end."

"I know. And she's completely different from the blondes and brunettes around."

Jo Ellen, always ready to support her enthusiastic cousin, thought about the girl. It was true she was incredibly striking. After a moment, she asked Natasha, "Don't you think she looks like Rhonda?"

"You know, I was just thinking the same thing." Natasha shook her head sorrowfully. "What a pity. I had high hopes for her."

The women turned away from each other and gazed ahead as the limousine continued along the parkway. Their faces changed from earnest excitement to dismay as they thought about Rhonda's grisly murder. Eventually Jo Ellen turned back to Natasha. "The fashion world is definitely missing something, don't you think?"

"Yes, but they just don't know it," Natasha said.

"So what's your plan, Nat?"

"Simple. I think we should try turning her into a famous model, just like we wanted to do with Rhonda."

"You do, do you?" Jo Ellen asked teasingly.

"Think about it, Jo. Her coloring is perfect for all of the fall fashions."

"True."

"And the magazines are shooting their November issues next month. The timing is perfect," Natasha said, realizing how clever she was.

"Yes, but Nat, seriously, how can we possibly get her ready to model so quickly?"

Natasha, never one to be discouraged, replied, "It's only July 2nd. Piece of cake."

"You really think so?"

"Sure. You're talking about Top Form Management—that's what we do."

⋏

Early the next morning, Natasha bustled down the elegant winding staircase of her Greenwich country home dressed in chic white cotton summer trousers, a red T-shirt and Gucci loafers.

"Good morning, Jo. Did you sleep well?" she asked as she walked into the large country-style kitchen.

Jo Ellen, wrapped in a white cotton terry bathrobe, was seated at the kitchen table drinking a cup of coffee and enjoying a cream cheese slathered bagel. She turned away from the gorgeous view she had been staring at through the bay window.

"I did, thanks. I still can't get over how amazing your house is. You're very lucky your parents left you this. I just love it."

"So do I. I can't wait to come here on the weekends. It's such a break from New York City."

Turning back to the window, Jo Ellen exclaimed, "Oh, look! There's a deer. Did you see that? I tell you, I could sit here all day and stare out the window at this amazing view. You know what?"

"What?" Natasha poured herself a cup of coffee.

"*Vogue* needs to do a photo shoot right here."

"You're right," Natasha said coyly. "And they need to use that beautiful girl we saw yesterday."

"That's a great idea, but seriously, Nat, she works at a produce stand."

Natasha sat down next to Jo Ellen. "Why do you think I'm up and ready to go out so early?"

"Let me guess. You're going to try to talk that beautiful redhead into becoming a model."

"Of course I am. You know me."

"Yes, you're my cousin; I know you pretty well."

"So you know I always go after what I want." Natasha sipped her coffee and smiled smugly.

Just one year younger than Natasha and close to her since childhood, Jo Ellen did know her cousin well, and knew Natasha was never one to pass on a great opportunity. She loved challenges and she fully believed in the strength of women. She was what one might even call a feminist. Jo Ellen adored her and put all of her energy into nurturing Natasha and Natasha's models, many of who came from all over the world to model in New York City at a very young age.

"And your plan is?" Jo Ellen asked.

"Well, it's simple. I'm going to introduce myself and convince that stunning young redhead she has what it takes to become a superstar."

"You really think it'll be that easy? What about convincing her parents?"

"Oh, you worry too much about the details. I'll work it all out. Just wait and see."

"OK, if you say so."

Natasha walked over to the counter and put her coffee cup in the sink. "Listen, if my weekend guests arrive early, be a dear and open a bottle of bubbly for them, OK?"

"Of course I will. I'll even get a head start and open a bottle now."

"Ever the party girl," Natasha said, laughing. She knew full well that Jo Ellen didn't drink alcohol. "See you later."

"Good luck."

Ready for her mission, Natasha called out for her driver as she walked toward the mudroom. "Sergio? Where are you?"

Sergio swiftly appeared from around the corner. "Yes, ma'am?"

"We're going back to the produce stand," Natasha said, grabbing her purse and hurrying out the door.

λ

"Here we are, ma'am," Sergio said as the limo came to a stop in the dirt parking lot.

"Super."

Sergio jumped out and opened Natasha's door.

"I may be a while. I have some business to take care of." Natasha fluffed up her hair, grabbed her handbag and slid out of the back seat.

"No problem. I'll just move the limo under the shade."

"Good idea."

Natasha walked over to the young redhead, who had just finished up with a customer. "Hi there. Can I speak with you for a few minutes?"

"Of course. How can I help you?" Anna asked, slightly perplexed.

Looking Anna in the eye and coming straight to the point, Natasha said, "Have you ever thought of becoming a model?"

Anna's eyes opened wide in surprise. "Me?"

"Yes, you. You're gorgeous."

Anna, bashful at such attention, looked down at the ground in embarrassment. "Thank you, but—"

"Seriously. You have the right height, the right weight and your features are not only perfect, they're totally unique."

"Really?"

"Yes really. Of course, we'd have to make sure the camera picks up what I see, but I'm quite sure it will. I've been doing this a long time."

Anna was surprised at this woman's interest. She didn't think she was particularly attractive. Although she was aware people stared at her frequently, she thought it was mostly due to her unusual red hair, which had been the butt of many nasty jokes in school. Anna listened as Natasha told her what becoming a fashion model would entail, even though she knew it was just a dream and far from her reality. She needed to take care of her brother and stay close to her family. But, on second thought, could this woman be serious? Could she really become a model and make enough money to help her little brother?

Overhearing the surprising conversation, Anna's grandfather turned toward Anna and accidentally knocked over an entire bushel of apples. "Porca miseria!" he said, swearing in Italian. Angry at his own clumsiness, he lifted up his hands in disgust and walked over to Natasha.

"What are you two talking about?" Carmelo asked in heavily accented English. "Anna, is this woman bothering you?" he said, looking from Anna to the woman.

"No, Nonno. This is—"

Natasha extended her hand to Carmelo before Anna could finish. "Hi, I'm Natasha Burns."

Skeptical, Carmelo shook Natasha's hand. "Carmelo Gallo, Anna's grandpa. Why are you so interested in her?"

"Well, Carmelo, I was asking your granddaughter if she had ever considered becoming a fashion model."

"A model?"

"Yes. You see, I own Top Form Management. We're one of the leading modeling agencies in the world. I think your granddaughter could—"

Anna's petite grandmother, Maria, walked over, interrupting the conversation. "What are you talking about?" she asked her husband sharply in Italian.

Natasha, not the least bit put off, offered her hand to Maria. "Hello, you must be …"

Wary from years in America as a poor Italian immigrant, Maria refused Natasha's outstretched hand. "Anna's grandmother. What do you want with her?"

Natasha immediately realized this woman was going to be difficult to convince, but didn't hesitate a second. "I was just telling your husband how I could make your granddaughter into a successful fashion model."

"Model?" Maria was dumbstruck. Of course she had noticed her granddaughter's striking beauty—you couldn't miss it—and of course she wanted better for Anna, but she had never imagined such an offer.

"Yes, a model," Natasha continued.

"Bah. You can't be serious," Maria said.

"Of course I am, Mr. and Mrs. Gallo. I know this seems like an outlandish offer, but I would take good care of …"

"Anna. Anna McKenna," Anna piped in eagerly.

Anna's grandparents glanced at Anna, then looked over at Natasha skeptically. Turning to each other, they began a heated conversation accompanied by waving arms and lively hand gestures. Natasha, a bit concerned about the upheaval, quietly observed.

"Don't worry, they're not fighting," Anna said, smiling at Natasha. "It's just how they communicate."

"That's a relief. I was getting worried. The last thing I wanted to do was start an argument between all of you."

"No, no, it's quite normal. They're from Sicily. They're very emotive."

"Emotive?" Natasha was impressed. Not only was this lovely girl beautiful, she seemed to be well spoken and quite intelligent too. "I take it you speak Italian?"

"I do."

"Are you from Italy then?"

"No, I'm American, but my mother was Italian." Anna looked at the ground sadly, unaware Natasha was gazing at her extraordinarily long eyelashes.

Before Natasha could comment on Anna's mother, Maria turned to Anna.

"Anna, tu, cosa pensi di questa signora?"

Anna brightened up. Her grandparents wanted to know what she thought about Natasha, which meant they were considering her offer. Bubbling over with excitement, she started speaking to her grandparents about the possibility of becoming a model, something she never dreamed could happen to her.

"So, you are serious?" Maria said, turning to Natasha.

"Absolutely serious. I would take your granddaughter under my wing, protecting her and guiding her as she breaks into the business. Your granddaughter has something very special, and I really believe in my heart of hearts that I can give her a life ... well, a life unexpected shall we say."

⋏

Natasha entered the front door of her white-trimmed, gray stone Greenwich mansion and spotted through the living room windows the pre-July 4th afternoon cocktail party taking place out back.

I must hurry. It's my party after all, she thought, bounding up the stairs. As she walked through the elegantly appointed hallway to her bedroom, she spotted the silver framed photograph of her parents on the hall table. She picked it up and smiled sadly. "How I miss you both," she said. *If you could see me now, I think you'd be so proud.* She kissed the photo lovingly, put it back down and hurried into her bedroom.

The red and white floor-length shift she had chosen earlier hung gloriously on a high hook in her walk-in closet. She changed into it quickly, slipped on her coordinating sandals and walked over to her silver mirrored makeup table. In one quick motion, she twisted her hair back into a loose chignon. She reached for her signature red lipstick and expertly dabbed it on. A gentle smack of her lips, a spritz of perfume, and she was ready. A feeling of exhilaration came over her as she walked past the bay window and glanced down at her guests. The crème de la crème of the fashion world were mingling together at her Greenwich home.

"I'm one lucky lady," she said as she descended the staircase.

She walked through her sumptuously decorated living room out onto the marble-tiled patio overlooking an expansive landscape of slumbering hills dotted with an abundance of woodland. As the sun began its descent, staff dressed in black trousers and white shirts passed trays of champagne and hors d'oeuvres amongst the guests. She spotted Jo Ellen and grabbed a flute of champagne before slinking up to her and whispering in her ear. "It's done."

"No way!" Jo Ellen stared at Natasha in disbelief. "You convinced her to become a model just like that?"

"Actually, I convinced her grandparents—the two older people there."

"What about her parents?"

"Turns out they're dead. She and her brother live with their grandmother and grandfather."

"Oh. So sad. Anyway, I'm impressed. How did you do it?"

"Well, it wasn't easy, but eventually I talked them into it. They're coming for a visit to see the modeling agency and my home next week." Natasha took a healthy sip of champagne. "I assured them that she will live with me and that I will take good care of her while she learns the ropes of the business. They were very skeptical at first, but Anna—our new girl's name—loved the idea."

"She did?" Jo Ellen asked, stuffing a piece of cheese in her mouth.

"She did. She begged her grandparents to let her try. Turns out she just graduated from high school and needs to find something to do."

"And they agreed just like that?"

"Well, I think the grandparents, who are from Italy by the way, can't afford to pay for college and probably don't want her to work at the produce stand for the rest of her life, so they did. More or less."

"You didn't tell them about Rhonda did you?" Jo Ellen asked.

"Are you kidding? Of course not!" Natasha looked shocked at the suggestion.

"Poor Rhonda. I really loved her," Jo Ellen said sadly as the conversation took on a somber tone.

"Everybody did. Such a tragedy. I hope they catch the scumbag who raped and killed her." Natasha was enraged that one of her special girls came to such a horrible end.

"Don't we all," Jo Ellen agreed.

"Just eighteen years old, and so beautiful. I want to cry all over again," Natasha said.

"So do I. She was such a sweet thing."

"So naïve though." Natasha shook her head.

"I wonder if she knew her killer. I mean, how did he get into her apartment?"

"Well, she must have let him in," Natasha surmised. "They say there were no signs of forced entry."

"Hmmm. As you said, so naïve," Jo Ellen said.

"Exactly. I tell the girls over and over not to trust anyone. There are so many creeps walking around New York City. I just wish I had gotten the chance to tell Rhonda."

Taking more hors d'oeuvres from a passing waiter's tray, Jo Ellen stuffed another one into her mouth. "Do you think the killer could have been that guy who was telling everybody he's the son of that famous photographer?"

"You mean Dennis Dunbar?"

"Right, him. The weirdo who calls himself Don Dunbar."

"Possibly. I hadn't thought about him," Natasha said.

"Well, he's crazy enough to have done it. He clearly gets his kicks out of beating up models."

"You think so?"

"Yes. Don't you remember he put that model, Jasmine, in the hospital? Maybe he graduated to murder," Jo Ellen said.

Natasha took another sip of champagne. "I thought he was in jail though."

"Don't know. Anyway, I'm sure the NYPD's doing everything they can to find out who the killer is," Jo Ellen said.

A tall, lanky, effeminate man dressed in red, white and blue swaggered over to the pair. "Ladies, there you are," the flamboyant guest exclaimed, putting an end to their conversation.

CHAPTER 3

Spartan Warrior

Detective Tansey opened the door of the small interrogation room and walked in. A tall, attractive guy with a blonde beard and moustache sat slouched in a folding chair, his elbows on the white table, head falling listlessly forward into the palms of his hands as he waited in disbelief. He was completely exhausted.

"Paul, my name's Detective Tansey." He grabbed the remaining folding chair and sat down. "I'm gonna ask you a few more questions about the weekend of April 14th."

Paul looked up at Tansey with exasperation. "I already told the other detectives who brought me down here everything I know."

"Unfortunately, we have to go through it again. In case you missed something."

"I didn't miss anything. I have nothing else to say." Paul crossed his arms and sighed. "I can't believe I'm here and you actually think I murdered this girl Rhonda."

Tansey recognized Paul's type immediately. He was one of those guys who reminded Tansey of a Spartan warrior—blonde, muscular, chiseled face. Ego. The guy looked familiar, yet totally out of his element sitting in the small, bleak room with its appalling fluorescent lighting.

"We're not saying you murdered this girl, but we need to cross all our T's and dot all our I's, you know what I mean?"

"Right, right," Paul said, now resigned to further interrogation. He was beginning to wonder if they were actually going to throw him in the slammer.

"OK, let's start from the beginning. You met Rhonda at an audition at Top Form Management on Friday, April 14th. Then what happened?"

"As I said to the other detectives, we started talking and then we agreed to meet up at the coffee shop around the corner after the audition."

"So you liked her?"

"Well, yeah, I guess so. She was a brand-new model, had just joined the agency. You know, she was like a fish out of water, so shy and intimidated."

"And you thought you could help."

"Yeah. Exactly. I just wanted to protect her a bit and show her the ropes."

"Right, show her the ropes."

"Well, I've been in the business awhile, so I know the ins and outs. I know a lot of important people."

"I see. Take her under your wing and help her make it."

"Exactly," Paul said.

"I get that. So then what?" Tansey asked sympathetically.

"Well, we had coffee and something to eat." Paul started to relax. He sensed Tansey understood.

"What'd ya talk about?"

"You know, about our backgrounds and stuff. She told me about her family and growing up in Wisconsin. I guess she had a rough childhood and really wanted to get away and make it big as a model in New York City."

"So you talked about her childhood and then you went your separate ways?"

"Yeah, but I asked her to meet up with me later. This designer I model for was giving a big party at Studio 54 and invited me, so I asked her to come. She met me there, we danced, had a good time, and then she left."

"She left? You didn't go home with her?" Tansey asked, suddenly remembering where he had seen Paul before; he was the guy plastered on a billboard in Times Square in an advertisement for a famous clothing designer.

"Hey, I'm not saying I didn't want to, but I'm not a sleazebag. I respect women."

"So she left by herself?"

"Yeah, she left by herself. I mean, I offered to accompany her home in a taxi, but she refused. So I told her I'd call her next week."

"OK, so then what did you do?"

"Caught the train."

"You did?"

"Yeah. I needed to head back to Queens for the weekend. My mom asked me and my friend Danny to do some work around her house, so I went there to help out."

"For the whole weekend?"

"Yes, for the whole weekend. I have a big family. I like to hang out with them."

"Alright, give me their phone numbers," Tansey said, taking out his weathered notebook and scribbling them down as Paul rattled them off. Tansey looked back at Paul. "OK, what about the party you were at? Did you talk to anyone else after she left?"

"Yeah, Danny showed up and we hung out there for a little longer. Then we left together 'cause we had to get the last train out of Manhattan before it shut down for the night."

"And you didn't go over to Rhonda's apartment first?"

"Detective, I don't even know where she lived. She never told me and I never asked." Completely distressed, he put his elbows back on the table and lay his head in the palms of his hands once more. "Jeez, I can't believe this is happening."

"Wait here while I make a few phone calls." Tansey got up and left the interrogation room. An hour later he returned to find Paul slouched over the table, crying. The guy who looked like a Spartan warrior was sobbing like a baby.

"OK, your alibi checks out. You can leave." Tansey held the door open while Paul stood up, wiped his nose and left the room. Tansey knew in his heart this guy probably wasn't the killer, but then again he could just be a hell of a great actor. Best to keep an eye on him.

CHAPTER 4

A LIFE UNEXPECTED

A sleek black limousine edged near the corner of 68th Street and Park Avenue in New York City and parked in front of an imposing townhouse. Natasha's driver, Sergio, stepped out of the limo and opened her door.

"We're here," Natasha said, turning to Anna while gathering her bags.

"This is your home?"

"It is indeed," Natasha said, smiling at Anna.

Anna peered out the window and gazed at the swank Beaux-Arts style building. She had never seen anything like it. The magnificent four-story white stone façade held court amongst a row of impressive townhouses.

"It's lovely," Anna said casually, attempting to hide her astonishment. Although her grandparents had told her about Natasha's home, she didn't expect this. Her eyes focused on the two Wintergreen boxwood shrubs potted in glazed, charcoal-colored urns flanking the entryway. "Wow," she said to herself as Natasha exited the limo and headed up to the black lacquered front door. Anna continued gazing at the four stories of black trimmed windows highlighted by billowy white curtains until Sergio interrupted her trance by opening the car door. "Thank you," was all she could say as she took her handbag and swiftly slid out of the limousine.

She caught up to Natasha just as the front door opened. An attractive, small Filipino woman with shiny black hair pulled back in a bun and dressed in a pink and white maid's uniform appeared.

"Hello, Nelda, meet our newest discovery, Anna," Natasha said to the woman.

"It's nice to meet you," Nelda said, shaking Anna's delicate hand.

"Nice to meet you too," Anna said shyly.

"Anna, Nelda is our dedicated housekeeper and cook. Believe me when I tell you that without Nelda I'm afraid I would be lost in my own home."

Nelda laughed. "Ms. Burns, you are most certainly exaggerating."

"Nelda, please show Anna to her room and introduce her to the other models."

"Of course. Come with me, Anna. Don't worry about your suitcase, we'll bring it up to you later."

Nelda led the way through the grand foyer. Anna's eyes skimmed over the black and white marble tiled floor and up the elegant spiral staircase flanked by black wrought iron balustrades as she followed Nelda. When they reached the third floor, Nelda led the way down a hallway carpeted with a Persian runner and through a molded, white paneled door.

Beyond, the classically elegant atmosphere changed. The Persian carpet was replaced by a fluffy, hot-pink shag rug, lending a funky edge to modern, fluorescent lime-green, white and silver wallpapered walls. Anna could hear female banter and laughter emanating from a door ajar on the right.

"Come, I will introduce you to your new roommates," Nelda said, stopping briefly and knocking on the door. "Ladies?" she said, before walking into the room. "This is Anna, your new roommate.

Please show her around and get to know each other, but remember to come down for dinner in an hour." Nelda smiled at Anna and disappeared out the door.

"Hey!" A tall, platinum blonde in a pink, flowered peasant dress jumped up and hugged Anna. "I'm Petra. So nice to meet you!"

Instinctively Anna hugged her back. "Nice to meet you too." She smiled shyly and quickly put her hands in her jeans pockets.

"I'm Anika," a young woman dressed in sky-blue spandex leggings and a matching tube top said with an accent. She smiled warmly at Anna as she continued lying back on a twin bed, her head of black, curly, long hair splayed out on pink pillows. Anna smiled back at the leggy woman with golden brown skin highlighting her dark chocolate eyes.

A striking young Asian woman dressed in simple khaki shorts and a white buttoned-down shirt raised her hand to say hello. "I'm Sue." She sat casually on one of two large pink and lime-green beanbags, her long thin legs crossed. "Come sit down next to me," Sue said, patting the other beanbag. "So, where are you from?"

"Port Chester," Anna replied

"Where is that?" Petra asked.

"Right near the border of Connecticut and New York."

"Well you certainly didn't have to come far," Sue said.

Petra, Sue and Anika laughed lightheartedly. Anna smiled. She liked these young women already.

"Neither did you," Anika said, looking at Sue.

"Not so, if you consider the fact I was born in Taiwan."

"Yes, but you're American now, are you not?" Anika asked. "And weren't you raised in Boston?"

"OK, you got me there," Sue said.

Anna, who had detected a slight accent when Petra spoke, turned to her. "Where are you from?"

"Sweden. That's why I'm so friendly," Petra said with a cocky smile.

"She is friendly, too friendly," Sue said in an authoritative tone.

"Come on now, ladies," Anika said. "That's what makes Petra so endearing."

"That's true too," Sue said, smiling at Petra.

"Where are you from, Anika?" Anna asked.

"Why don't you guess?" Anika said playfully.

Anna smiled at Anika. She was very beautiful and exotic, and she had an unusual English accent; one Anna had never heard before.

"Mmm. I don't have a clue. Are you from Africa?"

"No, not from Africa. I'll give you a hint. Tulips."

"Tulips?" Anna said inquisitively. Anika didn't look Dutch at all, at least as far as she knew. "Holland?"

"You're halfway there. Now the other half," Anika joked.

"She'll never figure it out. Even Sue couldn't and she went to Harvard," Petra said.

Anna looked at Sue, surprised. "Harvard University?"

"Yes, she's the brains," Petra said.

"But she left and decided to cash in on her beauty," Anika added.

"That's not fair. I was discovered," Sue said defiantly.

"OK, OK. We all were, so you're forgiven," Anika said playfully. "Anyway, there's nothing wrong with it. If you got it, flaunt it!" Anika turned to Anna. "You give up?"

"Yes. I don't have a clue."

"Saint Martin, down in the Caribbean," Anika said with pride.

"Really? That's exotic. I've never been there. Or anywhere really," Anna said.

"My Dutch father met my mother down there when he was on holiday and the rest is history."

"That's so romantic," Petra piped in.

"What about you, Anna?" Anika said. "You're rather unusual looking, not like the typical American."

"What's a typical American look like?" Sue asked.

"Like a Barbie doll," Petra said cheerfully, thinking about the two treasured Barbie dolls she had growing up.

"A Barbie doll? That's ridiculous. America is a melting pot," Sue said.

"OK, OK. Anyway, let's guess. You're Scottish American," Petra said.

"Good guess, but wrong," Anna said, thoroughly enjoying the fun she was having with her new roommates. "I'll give you a hint. I have Irish blood, not Scottish, but I also have Latin European blood."

"Latin huh? Well, she does have olive skin," Anika said to the other girls. She turned back to Anna. "Greek?"

"No."

"Spanish?" Petra guessed.

"No."

"It has to be Italian," Sue said.

"Si! Hai ragione," Anna said to Sue. "You're right."

"You're always right, Sue," Petra and Anika said in unison.

The conversation turned to their backgrounds and how they ended up as models in New York City. No one held back, each feeling a strong bond from simply being young, sharing a home and having had the good fortune of being selected by Natasha to come and work in The Big Apple.

"So, we were all given the opportunity to become models because of our uniqueness," Sue said.

"I guess so. It's amazing how life changes, isn't it," Petra said. "I still can't believe it. If I was in Stockholm, I'd probably be waiting tables."

"I'd probably be on my way to becoming a professor, just like my parents," Sue added.

"Well, I'd be married by now, with child," Anika said.

"With child?" Sue looked inquisitively at Anika, unaccustomed to such an expression.

"Do you have a boyfriend back home?" Anna asked, not fazed by the unusual expression.

"Yes she does, and he's a hulk," Petra said. The others stared at her. "Why are you looking at me?" she said.

"A hulk? Her boyfriend's not a green giant!" Sue said. "You mean a hunk."

"Right, right. I'm so silly. I mean a hunk," Petra said.

Everyone burst out laughing at the thought of Anika walking around with the star of the new TV show, *The Incredible Hulk*. Soon, they were out of control and in hysterics, rolling on the floor. Finally, after calming down, Anika turned to Anna. "So, what do you think Anna, did you ever expect to live in NYC in a mansion?"

"Never," Anna said. "I grew up in an old farmhouse. This is the last thing I ever expected." Anna was thrilled beyond belief. Not only was she about to embark on a career she never in a million years thought she could do, she also loved her new roommates and felt completely at home.

"I never expected to live in a mansion either," Petra said. "I grew up with my mom in a tiny apartment in the doggy part of town."

Sue turned to Petra. "Doggy?"

"Right, doggy."

Once again, the group broke out in hysterics. "Oh my gosh, Petra, you mean dodgy," Sue said, smiling at how her charming friend got so many English words wrong.

"OK, dodgy, not doggy. I do love dogs though," Petra said.

"Petra, we love you! You are so funny," Anika said, wiping away tears of laughter from her eyes.

Anna turned to Anika, curious about her childhood too. "What was your childhood like, Anika?"

"It was OK," Anika said, "but nothing like this. I grew up in a small town in Northern Holland."

"Yes, but now she's living with a boyfriend in a houseboat on a canal in Amsterdam," Petra said.

"Wow." Anna was at a loss for words. Anika sounded so grown up to her. She, on the other hand, hadn't even had a boyfriend yet.

"I miss him," Anika said.

"Why don't you go back then?" Sue said.

"Are you serious? This is my opportunity of a lifetime. I want him to move here."

"How's he going to do that? Doesn't he need a visa?" Sue asked.

"Yes, he does."

"Can he be a male model? You could introduce him to Natasha," Petra suggested.

"He's not the type. We have to figure something else out." Anika pouted, then brightened up. "Anyway, I'm going back at Christmas. I'm going to stay there a whole month."

"You are? But aren't we going to move into an apartment together?" Petra said.

"Of course we are, before I leave."

"You're moving out?" Anna asked.

"We are indeed. Now that we can afford it," Anika said.

"Right after we moved here, all three of us started working nonstop for Montgomery Ward's catalogue," Petra said.

"They pay a lot, so we have enough saved to move out," Sue added.

"Bummer! I thought I was going to have you as my roommates." Anna frowned, saddened. She liked these girls and had thought she was going to live with them for a while.

"Don't worry, Anna, we're not moving out yet," Sue said.

"Yes, and new girls are sure to arrive. Natasha's always discovering new faces," Anika said.

Nelda knocked on the hallway door. "Ladies," she said, peeking around the door.

"Oh my gosh," Sue said, looking down at her watch. "We're supposed to be downstairs for dinner already. It's chow time!"

CHAPTER 5

MAD AS HELL

It was the tail end of the dog days of summer. The scorching sun high-lighted the dusty air swirling around the produce stand as Maria and Carmelo unloaded the day's fruit and vegetables. Joey played with a truck nearby.

An unmarked police car pulled into the dirt parking lot. Maria and her husband stopped what they were doing and looked on excit-edly as their treasured son, Detective Mickey Gallo, emerged, leaving his partner behind.

Handsome, with dark hair and a striking goatee speckled with gray that only served to highlight his piercing green eyes, Mickey Gallo was the apple of his parents' eyes, and he adored them just as much.

But not today. Today he was angry and wanted answers.

"Ciao, Mama," Mickey said, kissing his mother on each cheek.

"Amore!" Maria said, expressing her love.

Mickey turned away from his mother and swiftly kissed his fa-ther. "Ciao, Papa." Then he put his hands on his hips and blurted out in Italian, "Can you tell me why you let Anna move to New York

City and become a model just like that, without even talking to me about it?"

Tension filled the air.

"Mickey, you were in Sicily. How could we have talked to you?" Maria replied in Italian, lifting her arms and shoulders in despair.

"Well, you could have waited until I came back before shipping her off to God knows where in New York City," Mickey said, tossing his arms out and raising his voice.

"Mickey, this is a great opportunity for Anna. We went there and saw with our own eyes," Carmelo said. He rested his weathered hands on Mickey's shoulders and continued. "You need to calm down, son."

"I'm not gonna calm down. I can't believe it!"

"Can't believe what? Like I said, this is a great opportunity for Anna. What's she gonna do anyway, work at a produce stand her whole life?"

"Of course not, Papa. There are lots of other things Anna could do," Mickey responded, exasperated at how naive his parents could be.

"I promise this woman, Natasha, is a good woman. We saw her home, her office, saw pictures of beautiful women, even pictures from Italy for those fashion magazines. You know, like *Donna* and *Amica.*"

"Oh, great," Mickey said sarcastically. "So you think Anna's going to be in fashion magazines just like that?"

Maria, wanting to defend their decision, tried to interject, but couldn't compete with the heated conversation taking place.

"I don't know, but this Natasha is a professional lady and she promised to look after Anna. Anna is even living with her and three other young women in her home. You should see it, so fancy, just like in the movies. I'm sure she is going to make Anna very rich." Carmelo was desperately trying to convince his son they had made a good decision.

"Papa, do you have any idea how many girls want to be models? It's a tough business, just like acting. Very few make it."

"Yes, but this woman told us Anna was very special."

"I'm sure that's what she says to every girl, Papa." Mickey threw up his arms in exasperation. "Give me this woman's address and phone number. I'm gonna look into this."

After scrambling to get Natasha Burn's information, Maria handed the torn out piece of paper to Mickey. Carmelo and Maria watched in confusion as their beloved thirty-eight-year-old son, a well-respected detective with the Port Chester Police Department, left the produce stand in a huff and sped away.

Mickey drove in total silence, leaving his partner, Bob, perplexed.

"What's the matter with you? What the hell are you so angry about?" Bob finally asked.

"I can't believe my parents let my eighteen-year-old niece pack up and move to NYC to become a model."

"When did that happen?" Bob asked.

"While I was in Sicily dealing with that Mafia ring." Mickey's fingers were bright red from clutching the steering wheel so tightly.

"You're kiddin' me, right?"

"No. Supposedly this rich modeling agent stopped at my parents' produce stand and spotted Anna."

"Well, you can't miss her. I mean, your niece is one foxy lady."

Mickey turned angrily toward Bob. "Hey, knock it off. She's only eighteen years old."

Bob, embarrassed by his outburst about Anna's beauty, tried to change the subject. "Well, what about your niece's parents? Where are they in all of this?"

"Where are they? They're dead."

"No shit. How'd they die?"

"Anna's mother was killed by a truck when Anna was only seven, and a few years later her drunken bum of a father collapsed and died of a heart attack when he was walkin' out of that bar, Jimmies."

"Holy crap."

"Yeah, so I'm like a brother to her, ya know? I need to protect her."

"I don't blame you, especially after that model was murdered in the Meatpacking District a few months ago," Bob blurted out, once again unable to hold his words.

The color drained from Mickey's face as he thought about the grisly details of the model's death, a girl who happened to be a redhead just like his niece.

"My parents probably don't even know about that," Mickey said, knowing full well his parents couldn't read the American newspapers and had no time for TV.

"Maybe not. Anyway, girls are murdered all the time. They don't have to be models."

"This is my little niece we're talkin' about. Like I said, she's a sister to me." Talking about it, Mickey got even angrier than before and started speeding. Eventually he slowed down—once he decided his next move.

"That's it, man. I'm gonna go to New York City and see for myself what the fuck this is all about."

CHAPTER 6

OODLES OF MONEY

"**B**ellisima! Gorgeous! That's perfect! OK, now turn to the side; I want to shoot your profile." Gianni Gavazzi, *Vogue*'s favorite photographer, clicked away.

Anna, a complete novice, did what the hip, handsome photographer told her to do and continued making different poses on the light orange backdrop. She still couldn't believe she was actually modeling for *Vogue* magazine.

Shortly after Anna moved to New York City to begin her modeling career with Top Form, Jo Ellen took Anna under her wing. She wanted to help Natasha make Anna a star, and so she took the risk and made a subtle sales pitch to *Vogue*'s editor about Top Form's latest discovery. It worked. Now Anna, swathed in the latest fall-colored fashions from around the globe, was going to be the featured model for *Vogue*'s November issue.

"Beautiful! OK! That's great, Anna. Next outfit." Gianni, sporting jeans and a T-shirt, swung his camera strap over his head, handed it to his assistant and walked over to the buffet table while Anna headed toward the dressing room.

"Anna, you look amazing. Do you realize that?" Jenny, the long, lanky makeup artist said as Anna entered the dressing room.

Anna rolled her magnificent green eyes. "Pleeeze! Don't exaggerate."

"By the way, a police officer—says he's your Uncle Mickey—is sitting in the reception area," Jenny said.

"Really, my Uncle Mickey?" Anna made a beeline out of the dressing room and rushed through the large studio over to the intimate and sleekly designed reception room. Peeking around the corner, she saw Mickey sitting on a black leather and chrome sofa, browsing through the latest issue of *Vogue*.

"Uncle Mickey, what are you doing here?"

Mickey jumped up, hugged Anna, and kissed her affectionately on each cheek. Completely taken aback by how she had been transformed from an innocent young girl into a beautiful young woman decked out in the latest fashions, he only managed to say jokingly, "I wanted to buy some clothes?"

Momentarily perplexed, she burst out laughing when she realized he was pulling her leg.

"Seriously, Anna, what are *you* doing here? You just pick up and move to New York City without telling me?"

"You were in Italy and it all happened so fast. My dreams are coming true. Don't you see? I'm going to be a famous model!"

"That's a dangerous business, Anna. Lots of bad things can happen."

"Not true, Uncle Mickey. I'm living with the most fabulous woman and—"

"I know, I met her. She seems very professional. It's just that you're now in the big, bad world." Mickey rubbed his nose as he pondered the recent murder of the young model, Rhonda. "It was much easier keeping an eye on you when you were living with your grandparents."

Anna haughtily lifted her head up high. "Yes, but I'm all grown up now."

"And what about your brother, Joey? I'm sure he misses you like crazy."

Relaxing her exaggerated pose, Anna took on a more serious expression. She knew her brother had learning issues and problems with his vision. Her grandparents tried to help him as much as they could, but money was scarce.

"I miss him too, but just think about it. If I can make enough money, I can help Joey. We both know that Nonno and Nonna can't afford to pay for any special tutors."

Mickey crossed his arms as he thought about what Anna said.

"Supposedly, if I make it big I can make oodles of money." She smiled as she crossed her arms, mimicking Mickey.

"Money isn't everything Anna."

"I know it isn't, but I love fashion. I love clothes. I just never, ever thought I would have a chance to do this. It's a dream come true."

Mickey put his hands on his hips in resignation. "Hope it doesn't become a nightmare."

"It won't. Listen, come with me. Let me introduce you to Gianni Gavazzi, the photographer."

"Sounds like a playboy."

"Not at all. His wife, Jenny, is here too. She's the makeup artist. He's famous, Mickey, and he's taking pictures of me for *Vogue*. Can you believe it? Lil ole me." She grabbed his elbow and led him into the studio.

"Hi, everyone," she said to the group mingling by the buffet.

Gianni and the rest of the crew, startled by Mickey, who was dressed in his police uniform because of an official event later in the day, stopped drinking coffee and munching on cinnamon buns. Immediately Rhonda's murder came to their minds.

"Don't look so worried, everyone. He's my Uncle Mickey. He's just come to check on me," Anna said.

Aware of the sudden hush that overcame the group, but knowing nothing about a model's murder, Anna cheerfully introduced the crowd to her wary uncle. Cautiously exchanging hellos, the group chitchatted for a bit, but no one dared bring up Rhonda.

Eventually Mickey glanced down at his watch. He had all the information he needed, for the moment. Anna was correct; Gianni Gavazzi, Natasha and Top Form Management were all reputable. He had no complaints. "OK, gotta run. Nice meeting you all."

The relieved crew shook hands and said goodbye.

"Let me walk you to the door." Anna hooked her arm through Mickey's and led him back to the reception area.

"By the way, Uncle Mickey, I'll be coming home many weekends to visit."

"That's terrific, Anna. Let me know and I'll be sure to stop by." Mickey held onto both of Anna's arms and looked straight into her eyes. "Be careful, will ya," he said, sighing.

"Yes, Uncle Mickey, I will," she responded, kissing him affectionately on each cheek. "Well, I better go change into my next outfit before everyone gets annoyed." She turned and raced back to the dressing room. Overcome with emotion, she didn't want him to see her cry. He was right, she did miss her family a lot. And she was scared—scared of the big, bad apple.

"Must be nice having a cop in the family," Jenny said, motioning for Anna to sit down in front of the makeup mirror.

The hairdresser and clothing stylist nodded their heads in agreement as they started prepping Anna for her next shot.

"It is. He's very protective, and smart too."

"Does he have a girlfriend?" the clothing stylist coyly asked.

The group broke out in laughter and the conversation soon shifted to men, love affairs and general gossip.

CHAPTER 7

DELUSIONAL

"So, you're the son of famous fashion photographer Dennis Dunbar, huh?" Detective Tansey asked, knowing full well the pitiful specimen of a human being sitting in front of him in the interrogation room was nothing of the sort.

"Yes, I am. And one day I will be just as famous as he is."

"Really? So let me ask you, why are you living in Queens with your mother and working at McDonald's?"

The young man who called himself Don Dunbar sat back in the folding chair, crossed his arms and looked up to the ceiling. He was indignant. He wasn't going to admit the truth.

Tansey grabbed Dunbar's shirt and pulled him close. "Look, you son of a bitch, I know you're just a measly little lying creep who likes to beat up models, aren't you? Speak up! Did you know the girl who was murdered? Did you?" Tansey was shouting as he pulled Dunbar closer. Dunbar, who'd gone the color of a tomato, started trembling. "You're pathetic, buddy, and you're not leaving this room until you tell me the truth."

Humiliated and caught out, Dunbar began caving. "Alright, alright. I knew her. I know all the models in the city," he said.

"Do you now? Tell me more."

"I asked her out once but she refused, so I let it go. I didn't kill her."

"So why is it you like to beat these girls up? I see from your record you were in jail for six months for smashing that famous model Jasmine to smithereens. Obviously, this is your thing, huh?"

"I'm working on it. I go to anger management every week. Listen though, you have to believe me; I didn't kill that girl. I'm not a killer."

"So you say. Prove it. Who are you really and where were you the weekend of April 14th?"

Resigned to having to confront the truth and let go of his distorted reality, Dunbar cleared his throat and sat up. "OK. I'm not Dennis Dunbar's son. My real name's Ben Fatniski."

"Fatniski?" Tansey suppressed his urge to laugh. "OK then, now we're getting somewhere. So, Ben Fatniski, tell me about your real family."

Ben put his head in his hands and sighed. "Real family? They're a bunch of losers. My mom spends her days on the couch watching soap operas, and when my dad isn't driving a garbage truck he's at the bar getting drunk."

"Go on." Tansey was enjoying himself now.

"So that weekend I was with my mom. I had to clean the house and then I went to work."

"Clean the house? Your mom doesn't do that?"

"No. I told you. She just lies on the couch every day and watches soap operas."

"Aha. And where do you work?"

"At McDonald's."

"At McDonald's?" Tansey said, clearly getting a kick out of this moment of truth. "So you flip burgers, huh? Seems a long way away from photographing beautiful women."

"Yeah, yeah," Ben said, sighing with resignation. "But one day, you'll see. I'll be a famous photographer and all the models in New York City will be my friends."

"Sure, Ben, sure. Anyway, you're saying that you didn't come into Manhattan at all that weekend?"

"No, I couldn't. I didn't have time. My mom made me clean the house all day Saturday and then, as I said, I had to work. Someone was sick so I had to do overtime that weekend to fill in."

"Give me your mom's and your boss's phone numbers."

Ben gave him the numbers and started to get up.

"Hey, sit back down. You're not going anywhere until what you say checks out."

Tansey left the room and called Ben Fatniski's mother. She confirmed that her son had been home cleaning the house on that Saturday. As Tansey hung up the phone, he noticed a TV was blaring in the background. Just as Fatniski had said, she was probably watching soap operas. She, too, lived a vicarious life, only with her it was through soap operas.

Next, he called the supervisor at McDonald's, who confirmed Fatniski worked most of that weekend because they were short staffed. Tansey, satisfied but determined to keep an eye on Fatniski, walked back into the interrogation room.

"OK, you can go."

Ben stood and looked at Tansey with a huge sense of relief. "I'm off the hook?"

"For now, but don't you dare leave New York," Tansey said. He didn't think Fatniski would, not as long as he lived with his mama.

"No, I won't. Promise," Ben said as he walked toward the door.

"Hey, one more thing, Fatniski."

"What?" Ben asked.

"Get a life."

CHAPTER 8

ANOTHER REDHEAD

Anna hopped out of the subway station on 59th and Lexington Avenue and headed north toward Top Form Management's office. In a terrific mood, she passed Bloomingdale's department store and peered into the fantastic window displays, daydreaming about all the clothes she would hopefully be able to buy one day soon. She turned the corner onto 63rd Street and slowly made her way to the agency, located smack between Lexington and 3rd Avenue. Passing the stately townhouses dotting one of the swankiest neighborhoods in New York City, she imagined what life must be like for its residents, many of whom were famous celebrities.

Reaching Top Form, Anna zipped up the stairs of the impressive brownstone and opened the front door. As she walked through a reception area filled with overstuffed sofas and armchairs perched on an enormous antique Persian carpet, the usual coterie of new models hanging about surreptitiously observed their latest competition. Anna, uncomfortable with the smoldering sensation of such jealous and competitive feelings, didn't stop to introduce herself. She quickly made her way to the large back office.

Four casually dressed female bookers were immersed in telephone conversations with the agency's clients. The atmosphere was frenetic as they feverishly took charts from the rotating center of a large white circular table, setting up dozens of models' schedules with the various photography studios, magazines and advertising agencies.

"Hi there," Anna said shyly.

Apart from Jo Ellen, the bookers, who intimidated Anna, barely acknowledged her presence.

Jo Ellen covered the mouthpiece of her phone and patted the empty seat next to her. "Anna, sit."

Knowing she would probably need to write down her schedule for the next few days, Anna sat, put her oversized black bag on the floor beside her, and took out her pen and diary.

"Right, I've got it. She'll be there at 8:45 tomorrow morning. Thanks and have a great day." Jo Ellen hung up the phone and turned her attention to Anna. "That was Dale, Donald & Frank, the hottest advertising agency in town, and they want to see you first thing tomorrow morning. They're casting for a Bling hair products commercial and think you could be the girl they're looking for."

"Super," Anna said.

Jo Ellen began dictating Anna's entire schedule of auditions for the next day and waited patiently as Anna jotted down times, locations and other pertinent information.

"OK, got it," Anna said.

"You sure? It's incredibly busy for you tomorrow. Word is getting around about Natasha's latest discovery."

"Huh?"

"I'm talking about you, Anna; you're the latest discovery. Don't you know that?" Jo Ellen smiled affectionately at this young new ingénue Natasha had such high hopes for.

"Really? To tell you the truth, I still can't believe any of it," Anna said.

"Well, believe it. It's true. All the top photographers and magazine editors want to meet you and take a look at your portfolio. You're on your way to being a star," Jo Ellen said.

"Crazy." Anna glanced down at her diary, baffled by all the attention she was getting.

"So, you know the ropes by now and how to get around the city, right?" Jo Ellen asked.

"No problem. I'm pretty versed in it at this point."

Satisfied that Anna had a good head on her shoulders, Jo Ellen turned her wheeled desk chair toward a shelf displaying individual 5x7 printed cards showcasing pictures and statistics of male and female models represented by the agency.

"By the way, here's your new composite." Jo Ellen handed Anna a card featuring test pictures of the transformed teenager taken by an up-and-coming photographer.

"Wow! I can't believe that's really me." Anna stared at the front and back incredulously.

"It's you alright. Here, take some," Jo Ellen said, handing her several. "Bring them with you to leave behind on each audition."

"OK. What time do you want me to phone in tomorrow?"

"Phone in around noon. Oh and by the way, Natasha told me to tell you that she was having a special dinner at her home for you and the other girls tonight. It's at 7 p.m.," Jo Ellen said while picking up an incoming call.

"Great. Thank you, Jo Ellen." Anna grabbed her heavy bag off the floor. Once she stood up, she took a moment to admire the wall display of the most gorgeous young men and women in the world. Amazed she was actually considered one, several moments passed before she snapped back to reality and headed out to the reception area.

Boom! She smacked into a tall, handsome, bearded young man, scattering all of her new composites on the floor.

"Oh gosh. So sorry. How embarrassing," Anna said as she knelt down to pick them up.

Seizing the moment, the sandy-haired young man bent down and began helping.

"Thank you so much," she said, turning red with mortification.

"Happy to help a beautiful lady," he said, a twinkle in his piercing blue eyes.

⋏

"I'm telling you, it was so funny. I was walking through Central Park—you know, where all of the roller skaters are—and all of a sudden this old man with long, shaggy gray hair wearing a strange purple tie-dyed outfit skates by singing at the top of his lungs." Petra laughed hysterically. "I mean, I guess this is New York, right? You would never see that in Stockholm."

Petra, Anika, Sue and Anna were in the midst of a lively conversation with Natasha while enjoying a meal served by Nelda. Natasha frequently had these special dinners for her girls in her elegant dining room decorated with sumptuously upholstered Chippendale chairs, fine Wedgewood china and silver cutlery. It was her opportunity to teach the girls proper etiquette. So many of them came from simple, even poor backgrounds and weren't used to the finer things in life.

"Well, in Amsterdam you would definitely see something like that," Anika said. "Anything goes there. You can even roller skate on the streets and smoke marijuana at the same time!"

The young women broke out in laughter as they imagined such a scene, but Natasha turned serious and took on an air of authority. "Girls, I grew up here and I've seen some real crazies over the years.

Not all of them are harmless either. Always remember to be aware of what's happening around you," she said before placing a piece of rare roast beef in her mouth.

Sue lifted her crystal wine glass filled with sparkling water and saluted Natasha as the rest of the group followed suit. Natasha was loved by all the models living with her, not only because she took them into her home, offering them a life unexpected, but also because she had such an amazingly strong, and at the same time loving, way about her. Each girl felt important and worthy, simply because Natasha took the time to care.

"By the way, Sue, tell us about the apartment you're moving into next month," Natasha said.

"Well it's in Chinatown, of course," Sue mumbled through a mouth stuffed with potatoes.

"Have you rented in a doorman building, I hope?" Natasha asked.

"No. There aren't any down there," Sue said. "Anyway, it's a safe area. And just think about all of the Chinese food."

"Yummy," Anika and Anna said.

Petra licked her lips.

Natasha turned her attention to Petra and Anika. "I hear you two have decided to rent a place together."

"We have. We found a huge loft down in Tribeca. It's so cool. I can't wait," Anika said.

"Me either," Petra said, smiling ear to ear.

"I don't suppose that has a doorman either?" Natasha looked at Anika and Petra with dismay.

"No one has one in Tribeca," Petra said.

"I'm not happy about that, girls. I know you are adults, but this is New York City," Natasha said, clearly disappointed, but knowing all too well how expensive New York City could be for these young ladies. They were just starting out and didn't necessarily want to spend extra money renting in one of the sophisticated doormen buildings that lined the streets of Manhattan.

"Most people are good people though," Petra said, looking at Natasha sweetly.

"It only takes one, girls." Natasha took another bite of her beef.

"Yes, but you've taught us so much," Anika said.

"We'll be fine. Anyway, I know karate," Sue said.

The girls looked at Sue with astonishment, as did Nelda, who had been busy pouring more sparkling water.

"Just kidding!"

Everyone cracked up, including Anna. As the newest model at the table, she had been listening intently, trying to learn as much as possible about her new city. The young women resumed eating and Natasha decided it was as good of a time as any to talk about the murder.

"Seriously, girls, I want you all to be safe." She took a moment to gather her thoughts. "I've been meaning to share something with you but wanted to wait until you got more acclimated to Manhattan."

The girls stopped eating.

"What is it?" Anika asked.

Staring straight ahead, Natasha grudgingly brought up the subject she had so wanted to avoid. "Do any of you know about a model named Rhonda?"

"Rhonda? Nope, don't know any Rhonda," Sue said, wiping her mouth with her napkin.

"Me either," Anna and Anika said simultaneously.

"Neither do I. Who is she?" Petra asked.

"You mean who was she," Natasha said.

Anna lifted a hand to her mouth in surprise. "She died? Poor girl. How?"

"Unfortunately, she was murdered," Natasha said.

The girls gasped as Natasha woefully looked down at her plate. "Yes, that's right. Murdered."

Stunned, the girls stared at Natasha in horror and disbelief.

"When?" Anika finally ventured.

"This past April," Natasha said after taking a moment to sip some water.

"That's not so long ago. How come we haven't heard about it?" Anna asked.

"I'm not sure why. It's true it hasn't had much press." Natasha looked momentarily bewildered. "Maybe it's because she wasn't famous. Anyway, the police are working on it."

A new, somber atmosphere blanketed the dinnertime chatter as the young models processed what they had just been told.

"Where was she murdered?" Petra eventually asked, breaking the silence.

"In her apartment," Natasha said. "The police think she may have known her killer because there were no signs of forced entry."

Anna's mind started racing as she wondered if her Uncle Mickey knew anything about this murder.

"Why would somebody do that?" Petra wondered aloud, not really expecting an answer.

"I'm afraid to ask, Natasha, but how was she murdered?" Anna asked.

The girls sat staring at Natasha, waiting to hear what they most definitely did not want to know.

"First, she was raped, and then her throat was slit."

The girls gasped in horror. Petra, always the most sensitive one, started crying. Anna's mind started working overtime, while Sue and Anika just shook their heads in utter disbelief.

"It's true. Such a terrible shame," Natasha said.

"What was she like?" Petra asked, dabbing a tissue to her swollen red eyes.

"Lovely, and stunning." Natasha turned to look at Anna. "She looked a lot like you—striking red hair and amazing green eyes."

The young women turned toward Anna with a sense of dread and pity, not knowing if the murder had something to do with redheads, models or just females.

"Oh, dear," was all Anna could muster.

"Poor girl," Natasha said. "She came from nothing really. But she desperately wanted to be a model. She told Jo and me that she just packed her bags and took a train to NYC. Unfortunately, she ended up renting a place in a bad area of the city. It wasn't until after she had lived there for a few months that she came to see us in the hopes of joining our agency. Jo and I immediately loved her look and were so excited about sending her out to meet potential clients. Sadly though, we never got the chance. She was murdered less than a week later."

"Really?" Petra asked.

"Yes, really," Natasha said wistfully. "That's why I implore you girls to be vigilant about the way you handle your lives."

"Well, we certainly will be now. Jeez, that's really terrible." Sue lifted her hands up in exasperation and dropped them back down with a thud.

"It sure is," Anika said, shaking her head.

Anna, thinking out loud, said, "I wonder if my uncle knows about this."

"Your uncle's a detective, right?" Natasha asked.

"Yes, in Port Chester," Anna said.

"Probably not then. She wasn't a famous model after all, so it didn't make headlines," Natasha said.

"Well, I'm definitely not going to tell him. That would be the end of my career if I did."

⚔

Anna stared out the side window of her uncle's 1970 Donnybrooke green Corvette, enjoying the last remnants of the orange and yellow autumn leaves bordering the Merritt Highway. She always had a warm fuzzy feeling in his car, with its worn saddle-colored leather seats and the rosary beads dangling from the rearview mirror, the radio always set to smooth jazz. Her uncle was like a big brother, always watching out for her, and now driving her back to New York City.

"I had such a great time visiting everyone," Anna said.

"So did we, Anna."

"Thanks for driving me back to Natasha's."

"Anything for my girl." He took his eyes off the road for a second and glanced over at his niece. "So tell me, how long do you want to do this modeling thing for?"

"How long? I don't know. I'm just getting started." She proudly picked up the November issue of *Vogue* she had in her lap. "Can you believe it? I'm actually in *Vogue* this month. That's a really big thing."

"Yeah, I know. We're all very proud of you, but I'm just thinking ahead."

"Well, I can probably model for about ten years or so. I'd like to land a contract with a cosmetic company or something so I can make enough money to help pay for a tutor and the eye operation Joey needs. It'd be fun to buy Nonna and Nonno some new furniture too. It's all so old," Anna said.

"You got that right; it's ancient. Listen, I wanted to speak to you about something."

"What is it?"

"You know, we hear things on the force."

"Tell me!" she said impatiently.

Mickey just came out with it. There was no way to soften what he had to say. "Last April a model from Wisconsin was murdered in her apartment in Manhattan."

Oh dear, he knows about Rhonda. Now what do I say? After a long pause, she finally settled on the truth. "I know, I just found out."

"You did? How?"

"Natasha told us at dinner the other night. It's a terrible story. Terrible," she said, shaking her head woefully.

"Anna, the bottom line is that you need to be very careful and on guard," he said, taking his eyes off the road momentarily while pleading emphatically. "They don't know who did this, if it's a one-off, or if he'll strike again. Models in particular could be at risk. Or maybe even redheads." Mickey was reluctant to say anything about the color of the victim's hair, but felt he had to in order to stress the need for her to be cautious.

Anna momentarily succumbed to a sickly feeling rising in her stomach, then took a deep breath and regained her confidence. "Don't worry, I'm always aware of what's going on around me."

"Good, Anna, you need to be. Especially in New York City."

"Do the police have any suspects?"

"I'm not sure, but I'm sure they're investigating every possibility," Mickey said, deciding at that very moment that he was going to get in touch with the New York City Police Department and find out a lot more about the murder.

"Do you think it could be someone in the fashion world?"

"Could be, or it could be anyone from a delivery guy to the tooth fairy."

"Well, you don't have to worry about me. I have no intention of getting caught up in the New York City party scene or anything like that."

"Good, glad to hear it. If you do go out to a disco or some-thing, don't ever go alone, OK?" He looked at her and waited for her response.

"Disco? I've never been to a disco and I have zero interest in going."

"OK then, I'm just sayin'."

Having gotten the subject of murder off their respective chests, they turned their conversation to the lighter things in life. Before long, Anna's favorite song, "Shining Star" by Earth Wind and Fire, came on the radio and the two started singing together, something they always did while she was growing up.

⅄

Mickey pulled up to detective headquarters in Manhattan and parked his unmarked black sedan alongside the other unmarked cars. He checked his watch, got out of the car, and took the stairs two at a time. He had an appointment with Detective Tansey and was eager to get to the bottom of Rhonda's murder story.

Walking into the headquarters, he noticed the usual setup: under-cover cops walking around, with one stationed behind a tall recep-tion desk.

"Hi, I'm Detective Gallo and I have an appointment with Detective Tansey," Mickey said as he pulled out his badge.

The detective confirmed the appointment in the diary on the desk then looked at Mickey's badge. After giving Mickey the once-over, he smiled. "Sure, man, right this way."

Mickey followed the detective through a hallway to a small office.

"He's right in there."

Mickey walked into the small room and immediately took in the strong smell of nicotine emanating from a butt-filled ashtray placed next to a pile of papers on a small white desk. A ruggedly handsome man of medium stature stood behind the desk and reached for Mickey's outstretched arm.

"Hi, Detective Mickey Gallo from the Port Chester police department," Mickey said, shaking the man's hand.

"Frank Tansey. Nice to meet you," Tansey said, sitting back down and motioning for Mickey to sit in the wooden chair in front of the desk. "What can I do for you detective?" Tansey took out a pack of cigarettes and offered Mickey one.

"No thanks, I don't smoke." Mickey said, wasting no time getting straight to the point. "What's the outlook on the murder this past April of the model, Rhonda?"

"Rhonda?" Tansey took a minute to collect his thoughts while he lit his cigarette, took a long drag, and blew the smoke out. "Word sure gets around, doesn't it," he said rhetorically. "Well, the outlook is dim. We haven't been able to find any significant leads."

"Nothing? No suspects?"

"We had a few. A male model named Paul, whose alibi checked out, and a nutjob who calls himself Don Dunbar."

"And Dunbar?"

"Real name is Ben Fatniski, but he likes to call himself Don Dunbar and pretend he's the son of a famous photographer. Like I said, he's a kook. Anyway, recently he did a stint in jail for beating up a model and now has a restraining order. I thought he could have been the guy, but it turns out he spent the weekend of the murder with his mom, and working at McDonald's."

"Huh. Anything else?"

"No, nothin' else. It's been seven months. We're movin' on now; orders from above."

"You're kiddin' me? Hell, a poor innocent girl was murdered."

"Yeah, I know. But you know how it goes. Happens all the time. What can we do? We have no more leads."

"I suppose you have some evidence at least?"

"We do—fingerprints, semen and hair. The fingerprints don't check out in our system. And I know I don't have to tell you that bodily fluids and hair are worthless unless we have a suspect to compare them to."

"I get it, but I sure would like to get to the bottom of this."

"Why do you care so much?"

"My niece started modeling is why. She's here in the city and I worry about her."

"Sure, I get that, but this was probably a one-off. Bad luck for the girl, but I don't think the guy will strike again. At least I hope not."

"OK. I'll try to live with that. Anyway, keep me posted will you if you pull a new scumbag off the street who could have killed that girl."

"Will do, but as I said we're putting it on the back burner now. We gotta move on."

Mickey stood up, unsatisfied, but understanding the system. This is how it worked. Nothing could be done about it.

"Nice to meet ya."

"You too," Tansey said, stubbing out his cigarette and shaking Mickey's outstretched hand. "Tell me, before you go, what's it like out in Port Chester? You come across a lot of murders?"

"Yeah, we do, but they're usually linked to the mob. Drugs, that sort of thing. Ya know, the occasional cement murder."

Tansey gave a weak laugh. "Must be hard getting a body out of cement, no?"

"Yeah, it is," Mickey said, nodding his head in agreement, "but they probably deserved it."

CHAPTER 9

CREEPS

By now Anna had a good feel for the transportation system in New York City. Although she preferred taking buses through the notorious grid, the graffiti-strewn subways were much quicker, and she managed to arrive at Richie Rubin's studio on 20th and 6th right on time. Noticing that the building was rather old and tired, she apprehensively buzzed the studio.

A loud voice came over the intercom. "Yes?"

"Hi, I'm Anna and—"

Zzzz!

She was buzzed in through the dirty, heavy glass doors. Thinking how icky the building was, she pressed the elevator button and, once inside, tried not to touch anything as it creakily made its way up to the 5th floor. She heard faint music, which grew louder with each passing floor. Stopping with a thud, the elevator doors slowly opened, revealing a dark, dank hallway.

"OK, what do I do now?" she wondered aloud, unable to see much of anything.

Cautiously getting off the elevator, she decided to turn left and walk toward the dull light and latest disco song, "Stayin' Alive," emanating from behind a slightly ajar door. She rang the doorbell and waited. No one came. Perplexed, she gingerly pushed the door open and eventually presumed she was meant to make her way into the studio on her own. Following the loud beat, she walked through a reception area and into an expansive studio, where an exhilarating scene unfolded before her eyes.

On set was a stunning brunette in a sexy, bright pink crocheted bikini embracing a chiseled, tan male model clad only in white swimming trunks. It was evident by the sky-blue backdrop that Richie Rubin was creating a beach scene. A fan was blowing the models' hair, helping to create a windswept frenzy of laughter, affection and fun for the editorial shot. Richie, a hip-looking skinny guy with shaggy brown hair, rapidly clicked his camera while the rest of the crew looked on.

"Fabulous. Great. Beautiful," Richie Rubin said to the models. "OK, let me see some love. Let me see some love, baby!" Richie eagerly continued clicking away while the two outlandishly beautiful models smiled, kissed and embraced for the camera.

No one noticed Anna. Becoming increasingly uncomfortable, she stood by the sidelines, unsure of her next move.

"OK, I got it. Next outfit," Richie said as he handed his camera to his assistant and the models danced their way off the set followed by the makeup artist and hair stylist. Turning away from the set, Richie finally noticed Anna.

"Hey, baby, how are ya? You want a coffee, a glass of champagne, whiskey? What can I get ya?" he asked loudly over the roaring music.

Taken aback, Anna eventually managed to squeak out a reply. "Oh, no, no, I'm fine for now. Besides, I don't drink."

"You don't drink? Hoity-toity are we?"

Anna didn't respond. *Terrified is more like it*, she thought while Richie stared her down. He finally broke his gaze.

"Anyway, the makeup room is that way. Why don't you make your way over there so the girls can work their magic. Not that you need any. You're foxy just the way you are," Richie said with a wink.

Anna shuddered. Naturally intimidated by men as a result of her father's explosively violent tantrums when under the influence of alcohol, she did what she was told. Entering the crammed, tiny, smoke-filled makeup room filled with fashion people, Anna noticed a long, thin makeup table strewn with cigarettes, coffee and champagne. A male model seated on one of the three stools in front of the table was hovering over a mound of cocaine piled onto a small, mirrored tray. He had a rolled dollar bill in one of his nostrils and was eagerly snorting a line of the white powder. Finishing with a long, loud sniff, he looked up into the wall-to-wall mirror, intimidatingly checking Anna out.

"Darling, you must be Anna," a thin, buff, gay makeup artist said as he stopped powdering the brunette model and femininely gesticulated for Anna to come in. "Aren't you a gorgeous one," he continued, eyeing Anna from head to toe. "Drop your bags and have a seat." He motioned to the one remaining stool and then turned toward the male model, now on his second round of cocaine, and said sarcastically, "Don't mind this one here, he's a party animal."

"Takes one to know one," the male model said, sniffing up his second line.

"Bitchy, bitchy, bitchy," the makeup artist said, sassily shaking his head.

Anna was totally taken aback by the scene. This was nothing like working for Gianni Gavazzi. All she could think of was how normal they were compared to this slovenly group.

Richie appeared from around the door. "OK, guys, let me have a hit."

The male model, still in his white swimming trunks, got up from the table. "It's all yours, man," he said, motioning Richie to sit down in front of the heap of white powder.

"Thanks, man," Richie said. "You know these hours. A man's gotta do what a man's gotta do. Say, why don't we all go to Studio tonight and boogie away."

Eager to please one of the hottest photographers in town, everyone expressed enthusiasm—except Anna.

Richie took a big snort of cocaine and then turned to the female model, who had just changed into her next outfit, an off the shoulder white linen peasant top tucked into a flowing flowered linen skirt. "Babe, you ready for your next shot?" he asked.

"Sure, how do I look?" She flirtatiously put her hands on her hips, swinging them side-to-side while looking seductively into his eyes.

"Great, babe, great. But let me fix your blouse." Richie got up from the stool and, kneeling on one knee, put both of his hands under her skirt.

"Oh, that tickles. Careful, you're getting a little close," the female model said.

Richie stood back up, took her hand and led her out of the make-up room, but not before turning back to the group and winking.

"Wow, is it always like this around here?" Anna said in disbelief.

"Darlin,' you ain't seen nothing yet!" The male model broke out in laughter, as did the rest of the group—except Anna.

Anna had just reached the telephone booth when the snow started coming down heavily. Ensconcing herself inside the dreary, graffiti-strewn glass box, she took off her mittens and searched for her agenda and a pen inside her enormous black bag. With frozen fingers, she dialed the agency and peered out, staring at the frenzy of Christmas shoppers making their way to Bloomingdale's. It was December 1st and the holiday atmosphere was palpable.

"Hello, this is Anna McKenna," she said shyly into the mouthpiece.

"Anna, you're just who I need to speak with," Jo Ellen said. "Congratulations! The advertising agency you just auditioned for already phoned to book you for their upcoming ad campaign."

"They chose me?" Anna said halfheartedly, a bit down in the dumps after her day at Richie Rubin's studio.

"They did indeed. You're shooting the stills and TV commercial the first week of January."

"OK. Great. And tomorrow?"

"You're booked with Gianni Gavazzi for Saks Fifth Avenue. You have a 9:00 a.m. start time."

She started to feel much better—she liked working for Gianni Gavazzi and his lovely wife, Jenny. "Oh, good," Anna said, managing a bit more enthusiasm.

"Also, you have a three-day booking with Richie Rubin for *Bazaar* magazine. They're shooting the pictures down in Jamaica. You fly out Monday, December 12th."

"Oh no," Anna said, unable to disguise her disappointment.

"What's wrong with that?"

Anna was momentarily unable to speak. Unsure of how to respond, she decided it was best not to tell Jo Ellen about her experience earlier that day at his studio. "I've never flown before," she finally managed to say.

Jo Ellen started laughing. "Relax, Anna, flying is a lot safer than driving. You'll get used to it."

"Of course, I'm so silly. I should know that."

"Anna, you're in such demand. Everyone wants to book you. You're going to be a rich lady soon."

"Well, I hope so, but money isn't everything, right, Jo Ellen?"

"True."

After getting the rest of her schedule, Anna hung up the phone, put on her mittens and grabbed her bag. As she headed over to Bloomingdale's to buy Christmas gifts for her family, she thought again about what Mickey said in the car when he drove her back into the city. Suddenly, in defiance, she blurted out loudly, "Maybe money isn't everything, but it sure makes life easier!" And with a bounce in her step, she made her way through the revolving doors.

The holiday atmosphere was breathtaking. Christmas decorations were everywhere, and Bing Crosby could be heard singing "Rudolph the Red-Nosed Reindeer" throughout the store. Anna made her way through the maze of frenetic shoppers to the escalator and headed up to the toy section, alive with excited little children scouring the area with gusto in search of the perfect toy to add to their Christmas list. Eventually she came upon an ideal gift for her little brother—an electric fire truck. After paying for it and having it gift wrapped, she took the escalator down to the women's section and made her way over to displays of holiday sweaters swathed in sequins, eventually deciding on a beautiful red sparkly one perfect for her grandmother.

Finally, she headed down to the ground floor and over to the men's department. She had two more gifts to buy, one for her Uncle Mickey and another for her grandfather. Spotting beautiful cashmere sweaters, she opted for a green one for her Uncle Mickey, knowing it would draw attention to his amazing emerald-colored eyes. She pondered what her grandfather might possibly like given that he only wore farmer dungarees. Eventually she decided on a plaid wool scarf. At least that would keep him warm when he drives his snowplow. She grabbed the scarf and piled it onto her arms with the sweater and wrapped gifts.

Trying to balance it all and carry her large shoulder bag—filled with a heavy portfolio, agenda, makeup and everything else a model needed daily—proved to be a challenge as she headed over to the cashier.

"Oh no, there's a line," she muttered under her breadth.

"You have a lot of stuff there, miss. Let me help you."

She turned to see a short, squat balding man dressed in a beige cashmere coat, wool scarf and brown shoes.

"No, thank you, I can manage," she said.

"No, seriously. I only have a tie."

Before she could protest further, he took the wrapped toy truck package out of her hands. "It's no problem," he continued. "Say, you're not an actress, are you?"

"No, I'm not," she said, surprised and embarrassed. Instinctively, she was now on guard.

"Well, you should be. You have a great look and I bet you can read lines very well."

"I doubt it. Anyway, I'm not really interested," she said, hoping the line would move quickly so she could pay for the gifts and get away from him.

"What a pity. You know, I'm a movie producer and I can make you a star."

Anna was speechless.

"Perhaps you've heard of me. My name's Alex Findler."

"No I haven't, sorry," she said, skeptical.

With his free hand, Findler reached into his pocket. "Here, take my card," he said as he handed it to Anna, forcing her to take it. "If you change your mind, give me a call. I'm working on a new movie. It's going to be big, really big."

"OK, thanks."

"Seriously," he said, doing his best to convince her. "You'd be perfect for the lead. You just need to come to my studio for a screen test so I can send it to the director."

Convinced more than ever that she needed to get away from this slimy character, all she could imagine at that moment was going to his studio and being murdered and then stuffed in a suitcase.

"Miss, can I help you?" the cashier asked Anna.

"Oh, yes, I'd like to buy this sweater and scarf," she said, relieved to turn her attention away from the sleazy man and to the cashier. Quickly paying, she grabbed her purchases and turned to head out the door.

"Hey, don't you want this gift?" Findler said, following her toward the exit.

"Oh right, I forgot about that. Let me take it." She tried to take Joey's fire truck, but everything started to slide off her arms and, before she knew it, Findler was escorting her out the door and into a taxi.

"Where to ma'am?" the taxi driver asked.

Distracted, she gave the driver her address without a second thought as Findler leaned in and handed the driver a twenty.

Rats. Now he knows where I live.

Peering into the backseat before he closed the taxi door, Findler winked at Anna and urged her to call him. "Remember, I can make you a star."

Although it was a short ride to Natasha's home, traffic was at a standstill due to the combination of snow and rush hour. Twenty minutes passed before the taxi finally pulled up to Natasha's tony brick town-house. Anna piled her purchases high onto her arms as she made her way out of the taxi and up the stairs to the imposing black door. She could see through the window that the others were already seated at the dining room table. *Darn*, she thought as she rang the doorbell. *I'm late.*

Nelda, dressed in her usual uniform, opened the door. "What on earth have you bought there, missy?"

"Hi, Nelda, I've been Christmas shopping."

"Well, hope you had fun," Nelda said as Anna entered the foyer.

"I did. I love shopping, but I don't love lugging all of this stuff."

"Here, let me take them from you and bring it upstairs to your room while you freshen up in the powder room. Dinner is being served soon."

"Thank you so much, Nelda, you're a lifesaver."

Anna hung her coat up, washed her hands and hurried into the dining room. "Sorry I'm late, everyone. I got tied up at Bloomingdale's. The lines were so long," she said, taking her place at the table.

"Not to worry, we're just getting started," Natasha said.

Nelda began serving a dinner of roast chicken, mashed potatoes and asparagus as animated conversation began between the girls.

"It's the holiday season and it takes forever to get anything done. Anyway, did you have fun?" Natasha asked Anna while cutting herself a piece of chicken.

"I sure did. I bought presents for my whole family. Bloomingdale's has everything!"

"I love Bloomingdale's," Petra said.

"Me too, although there was this sleazy guy there who wouldn't leave me alone," Anna said, delicately putting a tiny piece of asparagus in her mouth.

"What are you talking about?" Natasha asked.

"Well, I was having so much fun until the very end. Then this annoying guy waiting in line behind me started bothering me." Anna stopped there and took another bite of asparagus.

"And?" Natasha placed her arms, cutlery in hand, on the table and looked at Anna, waiting for an answer.

"He claimed to be a movie producer and tried to convince me that he could make me a star," Anna said.

"Huh?" Petra said in surprise. "Was he short, fat and bald?"

"Yeah, he was. He was really gross," Anna said.

"I think I know who you're talking about. I met him at Corner Café and he said he could make me a star too," Petra said earnestly.

Everyone stopped eating as the conversation took on an edge of excitement.

"Bah!" Anika burst out laughing.

"Right. Of course he can," Sue said with her typical cynicism.

"Who is he?" Natasha questioned, clearly not amused.

"Someone called Alex Findler." Anna took a big spoonful of Nelda's delicious mashed potatoes.

"Alex Findler? Never heard of him." Natasha thought about all the predators in the city targeting her girls and aggressively started cutting her meat.

"Well, I didn't think for a minute he was a real movie producer," Anna said.

"Really? I wasn't so sure," Petra said naively. "I talked to him for a while and then he walked me home."

"Are you kidding me?" Natasha was glaring at Petra.

"Don't worry, I never saw him again," Petra said.

"Thank God for that!" Natasha turned her attention to Anna. "And you, what happened?"

"He wanted me to go over to his studio to do a screen test for a director."

"And what did you say?" Natasha asked.

"Like I said, I didn't believe him for a minute, but he insisted on giving me his card and then, well, my hands were full and I was dropping everything, so he helped me into a taxi," Anna said.

"Does he know where you live?" Natasha asked.

"Kind of," Anna said, knowing full well that Findler had overheard her when she told the taxi driver where she lived.

"What do you mean, 'kind of'?" Natasha asked, more concerned than ever.

"Well, he overheard me tell the taxi driver your address."

"Darn!" Natasha turned to Nelda, who was about to serve seconds. "Nelda, keep the lights on outside all night from now on, and don't open the door for anyone you don't know."

"I never do, ma'am. Anyway, don't you worry; someone strange comes close to this house, I'll have the police on them in a minute!"

"I suppose you will, Nelda. It wouldn't be the first time you've invited them over."

Nelda nodded her head emphatically.

Natasha, resigned to the situation with this Alex Findler, took a deep breath, put a smile on her face and changed the subject. "So, on a different note, let's talk about the holidays. Don't you love this time of the year, girls?"

"Absolutely. It's so beautiful here. I love all the window displays in the department stores. And Rockefeller Center … did you see the Christmas tree?" Petra asked the girls enthusiastically.

"Yes! It's like a winter wonderland with the snow falling and everything," Anna said.

"I miss Stockholm. It's so beautiful at Christmastime," Petra said.

"Same with Holland," Anika agreed.

"We don't celebrate Christmas in my family, but I still like to get presents," Sue said mischievously.

The girls turned to Sue and laughed. Sue was just so straightforward, and they loved that about her. Tomboyish in all ways, her natural look was a bit deceiving because when stylists dressed her up and put her in front of a camera she became the most glamorous Asian woman in America.

"So, girls, I know some of you are going home for the holidays, but I hope you'll be back for Top Form's 20th anniversary party on January 10th," Natasha said.

"Party? I love parties," Petra said, talking with mashed potatoes in her mouth. She still had a lot to learn about table manners.

"What a drag! I don't come back from Holland until January 15th," Anika said.

"That's a pity. Everyone is going to be there—all of our clients, and even a few agents from Europe," Natasha said.

Anika, disappointed she couldn't come, thought about it for a second but realized she really couldn't change her plans. Nor did she want to.

"Where's the party?" Petra asked.

"Studio 54. Isn't that exciting?" Natasha, thrilled to have secured a private section in the most famous disco in the world, looked around the table proudly.

"Darn! I wish I could be there." Anika was having serious second thoughts, but knew it would be far too expensive to change the date on her airplane ticket.

"There will always be another party, Anika," Natasha said.

"I'm not really into crowds, as you all know, but I wouldn't mind seeing the one and only Studio 54," Sue declared, lifting up her arms and shaking her hands from side to side playfully.

Anna put her knife and fork down and sat silently while she digested the fact she was actually going to step foot in the most famous nightclub in America. Turning hesitantly toward Natasha, she said, "Do you think I could bring my uncle as my escort?"

Before Natasha had a chance to respond, Petra looked at Anna excitedly and said, "Yes, please! Bring him."

"Petra, all you think about is men. What if he's married?" Sue said, rolling her eyes.

Petra turned to Anna, "Oh no, is he?"

"No, he's single. He had a girlfriend, but they broke up a few months ago," Anna said

"So, he's available." Petra smiled. "I want to meet him."

"You don't even know what he looks like," Sue said.

Petra thought a second. It was true. She had no idea what he looked like. "He must look like you, Anna, right?"

"Not really. He's tall with dark hair and dark skin. He looks Italian. I mean, he is Italian. He has my green eyes though. Actually, I should say I have his green eyes. No, wait a second, we have my grandfather's green eyes. Oh, and he has a moustache and beard too."

"Wow!" Petra's eyes opened wide. "You see, everyone, he's just my type." Satisfied, Petra picked up her glass of sparkling water and took a swig.

Amused, particularly by Petra's exuberant reaction, Natasha finally spoke up. "Alright, alright. Generally speaking, the party is just for industry people, but I'll make an exception with your uncle, seeing as Petra is so interested."

"Thank you, Natasha," Anna said, reassured that she would have her uncle along.

"Yes, thank you, Natasha," Petra added, smiling from ear to ear.

"I so don't want to go to Jamaica with Richie Rubin on Monday," Anna said sadly.

She, Petra, Sue and Anika were delighting in scrumptious ice cream sundaes at Serendipity, a New York institution known for its particularly delectable desserts. It was Saturday, a day for treats. Natasha kept the girls on a fairly strict food regime—no junk food, candy or cookies—and instead gave them lots of fruit, vegetables and protein. She certainly didn't want the girls to obsess about their weight, but so many had lax eating habits and she wanted to teach them how to eat properly so they wouldn't have to worry about gaining a pound here and there. Of course, out of sight out of mind, and being typical young women, the girls decided to indulge and go to their favorite local hangout and splurge.

"Why not?" asked Petra, slurping up a big spoonful of ice cream. "You're working with Richie Rubin, the hottest photographer in town."

"So they say, but I don't particularly like him," Anna said, putting a spoonful of whipped cream in her mouth.

"I agree. I worked for him once and thought he was a real sleazebag," Sue said. "I think he realized how I felt. You know me, I can't hide it. Anyway, he never hired me again." Sue licked her chocolate-covered spoon and thought back to the moment she had given Rubin a dirty look, sealing her fate with him and his entire entourage.

"I've worked for Richie a few times. He's harmless really," Anika said with an air of confidence. She was two years older than the others and very street savvy.

Anna, Petra and Sue, on the other hand, still had a lot to learn. Even though they did their best to behave like mature women, they didn't have the experience that only age would give.

"I don't know, he gives me the creeps," Anna said. "Why is he so famous anyway?"

"Hello? His sister is the designer Rachel Rubin," Sue said.

"Really?" Anna exclaimed. "Well, I guess that explains that."

"Why don't you like him?" Petra asked.

"When I worked for him recently, he came into the dressing room and started snorting cocaine," Anna said.

"Cocaine?" Petra said.

"Yeah," Anna continued, "I was so uncomfortable because the male model was doing it first, and then Richie came in to do some himself.

"Wow," Petra said.

"And that's not all," Anna continued. "After he finished, he started flirting with the female model while she was getting ready for her next shot. Then he actually got down on his hands and knees and started putting his hands up under her skirt, pretending to fix her blouse."

Anika started laughing.

"Why are you laughing?" Anna asked.

"He tried the same maneuver with me," Anika said. "I just smacked his hands and laughed it off. I told him if he wasn't careful my boxer boyfriend would beat him up."

Petra looked at Anika quizzically. "Your boyfriend is a boxer?"

"No. Sometimes you have to tell white lies, Petra. You need to learn that."

"And that was it? He didn't get mad at you?" Sue asked.

"No. We all laughed," Anika said. "He didn't take it too seriously."

"You're so good at that sort of thing. I get really pissed off. I'm sure it isn't helping my career any," Sue said.

Anna turned to Petra. "So you've never worked for him?"

"No. I almost did though."

"Oh, what happened?" Sue asked. "Did you make him angry like I did?"

"No, not at all," Petra said. "Remember last week when I was booked for *Mademoiselle* magazine?"

"Yeah, but they cancelled you at the last minute, right?" Sue said, remembering well the day Petra found out.

"Right. He was the photographer."

"Oh, no. It was him?" Anika said.

"Yes, it was him," Petra said, her smile gone.

The girls shook their heads in sympathy. Petra, usually so sweet and cheerful, was often sad these days due to the constant rejection she was starting to confront. Suddenly, she was having a difficult time getting work because so many beautiful blondes had recently arrived in New York City from the Nordic countries. Swedish models, in particular, were the rage these days, and the competition was fierce. Natasha even had a talk with the girls about it. She said the business was filled with rejection and they had to realize the rejection could be for a number of reasons. The fact was, the girls had to toughen up since they were going to confront rejection constantly. She reminded them it was important not to take it personally, but to learn from it if necessary and move on.

"Did you ever find out why that booking was cancelled?" Anika asked.

"I think *Mademoiselle* thought I was too fat," Petra said.

"How do you know that?" Sue asked.

"When I went to the fitting, the clothes were tight. I could tell that's what they thought. I'm sure of it."

"You're not fat, Petra. Don't be ridiculous, you look perfect," Anna said.

"Thanks, but I feel fat."

"Oh stop it," Sue said. "Anyway, who did they hire to replace you? Do you know?"

"That Swedish model, Leah. She's much prettier than me."

"No she's not!" Sue said sharply. "You know how the business is. Anyway, maybe Richie had something to do with it. Maybe Leah likes to party and he wanted a model to party with."

"I didn't think of that," Petra said. "Maybe you're right. I'm still bummed out about it though. I mean, if you have magazine pictures from Richie Rubin and *Mademoiselle* in your portfolio it can really help your career. Right now, I need all the help I can get."

"True, but who wants to play that game," Sue said, stuffing a piece of cake in her mouth.

"Oh no," Anika said under breadth. "Don't look behind you."

"What, what is it?" Petra said, turning and doing just that.

"I said don't look," Anika grumbled through clenched teeth.

"OK, OK, but what are you looking at?"

"You know those two models from the agency, Alice and Sheila?" Anika said.

"Oh right, got it." Sue rolled her eyes. "I can't stand either of them. They're so full of themselves."

"Hi, Anika, who are your friends?"

Sheila had slinked up behind Petra, startling all except for Anika. She had such a whinny, contemptuous voice, so Anika, a good impersonator, whined right back.

"They're your newest competition, Sheila, so watch out."

Sheila, unaccustomed to meeting her verbal match, suddenly looked away toward the back of the room and said, "Oh look, Alice, our table is ready." She grabbed Alice and quickly walked away.

"I worked with her a few times," Anika said. "She's so snotty and stuck on herself. I mean, most girls I work with are really lovely, but every once in a while, a real spoiled brat comes along."

"When I walked into the agency for an audition recently, she stared me down like she had, she had ..."

"Daggers in her eyes? Is that what you're trying to say, Anna?" Sue asked.

"Exactly. She was so intimidating."

"I always strike back," Anika said. "Usually, they can't take their own medicine. I learned that a long time ago."

"You are so clever," Petra said.

The girls started chanting, "We want to be like Anika, we want to be like Anika," and laughing hysterically. Finally settling down, the conversation turned serious again.

"What about that girl Alice?" Sue asked.

"What about her?" Anika said.

"Well, she looks like the walking dead. Is she anorexic?" Sue asked.

"No doubt about it. Everyone knows it," Anika responded.

"Yikes, that's crazy," Petra said.

"Yup. Supposedly she just lives off coffee and cigarettes," Anika said.

Petra took an enormous spoonful of her ice cream, wiped her mouth and excused herself to go to the bathroom.

Sue leaned in after Petra walked away. "Speaking of anorexia, I think Petra may be developing a problem."

"Why do you say that?" Anna asked.

"Look, she just went to the bathroom, right?"

"So, she has to pee. What's the big deal?" Anika said.

"The big deal is I think she went to throw up." Sue was emphatic. "She keeps saying she's fat."

Anna didn't respond. She didn't have any experience with anorexia or bulimia. She hardly knew what they were since she was fortunate enough to be able to eat anything she wanted.

"I really am a little worried about her," Sue continued. "She's so sensitive and I think the fact work hasn't been falling at her feet like before is starting to make her nervous."

"Right, and now that we are moving into our own apartment and will have to pay rent probably isn't helping either," Anika said.

"I'm sure that's part of it, but maybe she's homesick too," Anna said. "Don't you both find it hard being away from your family and everything that's familiar to you?"

"For sure. Not only that, even though it's great living at Natasha's, it's a little uncomfortable, at least for me. I'm not used to such a swishy environment," Sue said.

"Neither am I, but it's been super. Anyway, in a few weeks we're moving into our own apartments. Hooray!" Anika said.

"Hush, here she comes," Sue said.

The girls changed subject and started speaking about their holiday plans, unaware a young man had parked himself at the table next to them and was listening intently to their conversation. Petra reached the table as he took a sip of his milkshake and then intentionally spilled it, some of which landed on Petra's jeans as she pulled out her chair to sit down.

"Oh man," he exclaimed. "I'm really sorry about that."

The girls turned to look at the brown-haired young man dressed in jeans and a beige Down ski jacket.

"Let me help you clean it up," he said.

Petra started laughing, or crying—it was hard to tell because she was so emotional. "Don't worry about it," she said. "I like milkshakes."

Everyone started cracking up. Smooth as a cat, the young man schmoozed his way into their conversation and before long sat amongst the girls.

"So you're models, right?" he asked.

The young women were used to being immediately recognized as such everywhere they went, even without their makeup. Besides being much taller than the average woman, they were simply drop-dead beautiful.

"What agency are you with?" he continued.

"Top Form Management," Petra answered.

"My father hires a lot of models from that agency," he said.

Petra sat eagerly waiting to hear more. Anna was curious, Sue was suspicious and Anika was amused.

"Who's your father?" Sue asked.

"Dennis Dunbar," Ben Fatniski said.

"You're his son? Wow, that's incredible." Petra couldn't believe their luck.

"Yes. I'm a photographer too. Usually I help my dad out, but now I'm breaking out on my own. In fact, I'd love to take some pictures of you girls."

The girls glanced at each other and paused before Petra spoke up. "You mean take some test shots?"

"Absolutely." Fatniski turned and looked intently at Petra. "What do you think?"

"Sure," Petra said. "I'd love to."

Ben Fatniski, a.k.a. Don Dunbar, had found his prey. He lost interest in the other girls. They were not so naive, but this one, this one was sold.

CHAPTER 10

HOME FOR THE HOLIDAYS

Anna snuggled under the covers in her old four-poster bed in Port Chester and thought about the booking down in Jamaica with Richie Rubin. *Thank goodness it came and went without a hitch*, she thought, as she relived the fun she'd had with the group of models and crew of twelve that had descended on the island for *Harper's Bazaar*. Feeling proud, she thought about how clever she had been in her efforts to dodge Rubin's come-ons until he finally left her alone and turned his attention to some of the more eager models.

I guess he lost interest because I don't like to party, she thought, unaware that he wouldn't have hired her except for the fact she was in demand and the editor of *Bazaar* insisted.

She looked over at her alarm clock. It was only 8:00 a.m. "Finally, I can sleep in," she said, pleased that work had slowed down, allowing her to return to her protective family cocoon and relax. Top Form Management had closed its doors for a few weeks for the holidays, allowing all the models to return home to visit family and friends scattered across the globe. She sat up, stretched out her arms wide and yawned. Then she plopped back down on the mattress, grabbed her book, *The Thorn Birds*, and once again snuggled under the covers to read. Before long, she fell back to sleep.

Half an hour later she slowly woke up, got out of bed and slid on her slippers, relieved she didn't have to get ready for auditions or bookings and hurry out the door. She put on her bathrobe and made her way down the creaky staircase and into the living room, pausing to look at the magical Christmas tree surrounded with several family gifts and a handmade nativity scene. Following the wonderful smells emanating from the kitchen, she walked in to find her grandmother standing at the kitchen table in her housedress. Maria was busy making tortellini in brodo, traditional meat-stuffed pasta rings in broth, for Christmas lunch the next day, while Joey, clad in his Batman costume, watched TV nearby.

"Ciao, Nonna," Anna said, shuffling over to her grandmother and giving her a kiss on each cheek.

"Amore mio," Maria said, forever calling Anna or anyone she held dear her love.

"Anna." Joey jumped up and hugged his sister, reaching little higher than her waist.

"Hey, honey bunny. You look far out in that Batman costume," Anna said as she kissed her little brother's head of curly black hair.

"I am Batman," Joey said indignantly.

"Of course you are, Joey, of course!" Anna said.

"Sit down, tesoro." Maria turned on the stove to heat up the moka pot of Italian espresso and a small pan of milk. "Macine?" she asked, smiling as she held up a bag of Mulino Bianco Macine cookies from Italy.

"Yes, please!" Anna smiled as her grandmother placed a bowl filled with the round doughnut-shaped vanilla cookies in front of her. Joey, now seated on Anna's lap, took a cookie and handed it to Anna, who gobbled it up in no time.

"Oh, how I missed those," she said.

The moka pot gurgled louder as the remaining drops of espresso boiled into the carafe. Maria took it and a carafe of hot milk, placed it next to Anna, and sat down.

"So how is life in New York City? Tutto bene?" Maria asked.

"Everything's great, Nonna," Anna said, trying to stifle the melancholic thoughts that were beginning to surface. She didn't want to tell her grandmother about her feelings of loneliness now that Petra, Sue and Anika had moved out. It was temporary after all since new models were moving in after the holidays.

"What about your work? Are you enjoying it?"

Despite living a life she had never dreamed of, Anna wasn't really sure anymore. Yes, modeling was considered glamorous and she had the potential to make a lot of money, but it had its downside, and it was hard work too. Not that she minded—she had been working hard her entire life—but she had always envisioned working at something more intellectual.

"I am. But I don't get to use my brain all that much."

"But it's so glamorous, isn't it?" Maria asked wistfully.

"It can be." Anna didn't have the heart to tell her grandmother how unglamorous modeling could really be. Many days were spent schlepping around New York City with a heavy bagged filled with her portfolio, makeup, shoes, and sometimes even a wardrobe. She seemed to always be running to auditions or a two-hour booking here, a three-hour booking there, or the occasional full-day booking.

"What do you mean, it can be? What are you hiding?" Maria said, looking at Anna suspiciously.

Anna thought about the last modeling job she had for a woman's clothing catalogue, just a week prior. Initially excited about the full-day booking because it paid well, she quickly changed her feelings when she arrived first thing in the morning and discovered that she had to work outside in the freezing cold. She even picked up a nasty cold after having spent the day running from inside a parked van over to a waiting photographer a hundred yards away, ripping off her heavy winter coat revealing summer clothes, posing for at least twenty-four frames, putting her coat back on and then running back to the van to change and do it all again.

"I'm not hiding anything, I'm just a little worn out. The trip to the Caribbean was tiring, even if it was a lot of fun," Anna said, determined not to tell her grandmother her mixed feelings for fear she would put a stop to her new career.

"I thought it was like a paid vacanza."

"It was sort of a paid vacation, but we had to get up very early to catch the right light," Anna said, unwilling to tell her grandmother about dealing with Richie Rubin and his antics.

The truth was, modeling could be physically and mentally exhausting, and it just wasn't as glamorous as people thought. Sure, there were glamorous moments. Heck, she was about to go to a big party at Studio 54. But she had to schlepp around the city, work outside no matter the weather, and on top of that, she also had to deal with people like creepy Richie Rubin, or that sleazy movie producer Alex somebody.

"Tesoro, nothing is easy in life, but now you can rest."

"It's good to be home. And I don't have to be back until after La Befana," Anna said, thrilled that Top Form didn't expect her back until after the Epiphany, on January 6th.

Joey looked at his sister with wide eyes. "The Good Witch won't bring me coal, will she?"

Anna smiled at her little brother. "Well, have you been good?"

Joey thought about it a minute. "Yes. So, Babbo Natale is going to bring me presents tonight, right?"

"Well, did you clean your bedroom?" Maria asked as she got up from the table and walked over to the sink.

Joey didn't answer. He slipped off Anna's lap, put his head down and started to fiddle with his costume.

"If your room is super clean, I think Father Christmas will bring you gifts. But, of course, you need to be very good this week if you want La Befana to bring you chocolate and a little present instead of coal," Anna said.

Joey turned and made a beeline up the stairs.

Anna and her grandmother looked at each other and burst out laughing.

"He still thinks there's a Santa Claus and a Good Witch," Anna said, shaking her head in disbelief. "I wonder if tonight he'll figure out it's Uncle Mickey who sneaks away to dress up as Babbo Natale and bring his gifts."

"Maybe not. He doesn't want to know the truth."

"But, Nonna, he's eleven years old."

"He's still young, let him believe. You still did at that age, Anna."

"No, I didn't."

"You pretended to anyway. You thought you wouldn't get any presents if we knew you didn't believe."

Anna scoffed. "I forgot about that. How ridiculous." She changed the subject. "So, how is Joey?"

"He's struggling. He's very immature." She looked to the ceiling to thank God. "Grazie Dio he was put a year behind. He would never have survived with the other eleven year olds."

"But is he learning?" Anna asked.

"He continues to have difficulties. He can't sit still. The teachers say he's hyperactive and should have special tutoring."

"All these complications from being born so early," Anna said, shaking her head.

"We're lucky he's alive," Maria said, making the sign of the cross.

"Oh please, don't remind me of that," Anna said, pushing out memories of her little brother's struggles to survive. "What about his eyes? What do the doctors say?"

"They are a problem. The doctors say he has something called high myopia and needs to be seen by an eye doctor regularly."

"Poor Joey." Anna shook her head in dismay. "Is there anything they can do?"

"They want to try an operation." Maria's mood changed. She put her hands together while looking toward the ceiling and pleaded to the lord. "Oh mio Dio, per favore, help my little grandchild."

Anna got up and hugged her grandmother. "Don't worry, it's all going to work out," she said. "I'm going to help too, as much as I can."

Maria rested her head on Anna and squeezed her tightly. "Sei un angelo."

Anna kissed her grandmother and resolved to stop thinking negative thoughts about her career and to concentrate instead on being the angel her grandmother thought she was. She had a mission—the one from the day her mother died—and she would return to New York and do everything she could to fulfill it.

La Vigilia, Christmas Eve, came and went with a flash, as did Christmas lunch and the subsequent games of tombola, much like bingo, and a few hands of the traditional Italian card games sette e mezzo and mercante in fiera. Anna spent the rest of the week helping her grandmother make even more food and Joey with his homework, then taking Joey and his friend sleighing at the nearby park. She managed to see a few of her school friends too, although many had started going their own way. It seemed she didn't have much in common with them anymore, and she sensed they were intimidated by her—word had gotten around about her new career and it left them a bit speechless. When New Year's Eve rolled around, Anna decided to stay home.

"Let me help you with that," she said to Maria, who was busy serving up zampone and lenticchie. Anna took the big plate of pig's trotters and lentils into the dining room and placed it in front of her grandfather, who was sitting at the head of the table.

Her grandfather smiled, breathing in the rising vapor. "Che buono," he said.

Joey looked at the plate of steaming hot food. "Do I have to eat pig's feet?" he asked, horrified.

"No, Joey, you get to eat cotechino," Maria said, overhearing Joey from the kitchen.

Joey looked at Anna with a worried look.

"Sausage," she said.

He smiled and relaxed. "I don't want to eat those little things though."

"What, you don't want to eat lentils? They bring good luck, Joey. La Befana," Anna said with a twinkle in her eye.

"And they'll make you big and strong like me," Mickey said.

Everyone laughed when Joey, once again in his Batman costume, flexed his muscles.

"Preghiamo," Carmelo said, requesting the family pray once everyone sat down.

Anna's grandfather took a moment to thank God for all of the family's blessings, in particular Anna's unexpected newfound success. Then he picked up an open bottle of Ernest and Julio Gallo's latest wine creation, Carlo Rossi, and poured some for everyone, even mixing a tiny bit in Joey's water. "Salute," he said, as everyone picked up their glasses in a toast. Carmelo put his glass down, closed his eyes and brought the fingertips of his right hand together and touched his lips. Kissing them, he let them burst apart in the typical Italian gesture of delight. "Buonissimo," he said.

"Nonno, it says Gallo Wines on this bottle. Is this our wine?" Joey asked.

"Not exactly, but the owners are my long-lost cousins. We must go to California to meet them," Carmelo said.

"Right, Papa," Mickey said. "Do you know how many people are named Gallo in the United States?"

Carmelo smiled at his son, knowing very well the successful wine purveyors were not long-lost relatives. He changed the subject. "So, Michelino, when are you going to meet someone and get married?"

"Si, Michelino, you're already thirty-eight. It's time," Maria added.

Mickey let out a sigh. He had to endure this conversation at every gathering he had with his mother and father. The last thing he wanted to do after breaking up with his last girlfriend, a nightmare, was to get into another relationship. He was perfectly happy dating with no strings attached. Besides, his career was demanding. "So, is everyone wearing their red underwear?" Mickey said purposefully, changing the worn-out subject of marriage.

Everyone looked at each other and started laughing. Joey's eyes opened wide and then he jumped off his seat and started to take off his Batman costume. He wanted show everyone that he was wearing his lucky red underpants.

"Don't worry, Joey, we believe you," Maria said. "La Befana will come."

"I don't have any friends who purposely wear red underwear on New Year's Eve," Anna said, looking from her grandmother to her grandfather.

"That's because you need more Italian friends!" Carmelo roared. "Everyone in Italy knows you have to wear red underwear on Capodanno if you want to have good luck for the year."

"Of course, Nonno," Anna said, smiling.

The family banter lasted for hours, after which they played cards, this time for pennies. The evening went quickly, as did the rest of the week, and before long it was time for Anna to return to New York City. Pleased with having had so much time with her family and lots of time to teach Joey many of the things little boys his age already knew, she was convinced more than ever that she had to deal with the sleazy side of the modeling industry and use the extra money she made to hire tutors and get her little brother into programs geared toward his special needs, not to mention, pay for an eye operation.

It was time to return to New York City and give it all she had to succeed.

CHAPTER 11

AN OPPORTUNITY

"**G**orgeous! Stunning! OK, we got it. That's a wrap. Thanks, Anna."

"Thank you." Anna was sitting on a cube on a white backdrop set up for the Bling hair products commercial. It was January 9th and the city was back in motion. A few executives from Bling, the art director and producer from Dale, Donald & Frank, and the crew had all been watching intently while David Arc, a well-known director of TV commercials, directed the filming of Anna as a fan blew her hair back off her face and she repeated her one line: "Bling—beautiful!" That's all she had to say to be paid $5,000 for the few hours it took to get it right, and that fee didn't even include the residual payments she would earn every time the commercial aired anywhere in the world. Her only obligation was to be loyal to Bling—she couldn't work for another hair product company for the duration of her contract. She was the Bling model, and would soon become recognizable as such throughout the United States or anywhere Bling hair products were sold. She had been hoping for a booking like this; it was where the real money was to be made.

The art director thanked Anna, David Arc, and his crew as the filming came to an end and everyone headed over to the buffet table.

"I don't know about you, Anna, but I'm starving," David said.

"Me too. First I need to call the agency though. I'll be back in a minute." Anna walked past the buffet table were many members of the crew were already indulging in a gourmet spread and chitchatting about their holidays, the weather, and the commercial that just wrapped up, and headed to the sleek, modern reception area. She picked up the telephone and dialed the agency, immediately recognizing Jo Ellen's friendly voice.

"Hi, Jo Ellen, it's Anna. I just wanted to check in to get tomorrow's schedule."

"Anna, you're exactly who I wanted to talk to," Jo Ellen said enthusiastically. "I have a question; do you have any interest in going to model in Italy for a few months?"

"Italy?" Anna was completely taken aback. She had heard through the grapevine that fashion models did go to work in Italy, Paris, Tokyo—all over the world really—but she didn't know too much about it.

"Yes, Italy. The tear sheets you would get could add a lot to your portfolio. Clients are always impressed when they see pictures from the Italian magazines. Even though you are already in demand here in the US, having the chance to work with some of the best photographers and designers in Italy, which means the world really, would put you on the international stage."

Flabbergasted, Anna took a few seconds to respond. "Never thought about it, but I do speak Italian."

"You do? Fantastic. Be at the agency tomorrow at 11:00 to meet Franco Rubelli. He's Italy's top agent and he's scouting for models to bring to Milan."

"Exciting. I'll be there!" Anna hung up the phone. Her mind was racing as she thought about the possibility of working in the country so dear to her heart. Her mother was 100 percent Italian. Anna spoke Italian. The grandparents who raised her were Italian. *What a fabulous opportunity.* But, could she convince her family? The smile on her face faded as she realized they would probably never in a million years let her go live in Milan for a few months, even if it was a country dear to their hearts.

⋏

An excited group of young men and women eager to have a chance at modeling in one of the hot spots of the international modeling world was waiting in the Top Form Management reception room for their turn to audition for Franco Rubelli, owner of Rubelli Models, one of the most important agencies in Italy—in the world, for that matter.

"Anna?" A booker appeared from the hallway leading to the small office were the audition was taking place.

"Oh, guess it's my turn," Anna said shyly to Paul, the male model she had been chitchatting with.

The handsome blonde haired, blue-eyed, bearded young man, who had helped her pick up all of the composites she had dropped in front of him only a month ago, liked her. A lot. There was a definite mutual attraction.

"Good luck," he said to Anna.

"Thanks, and you too." Portfolio in hand, she made her way through the crowd and into the back corner office, where she promptly tripped over the wood transition strip.

"Oh dear. Excuse me, I'm such a klutz," she said, quickly regaining her footing. By now so used to constantly tripping, she hoped it came across as charming.

Franco Rubelli, an attractive Italian man of medium build with curly black hair and dark brown eyes, was seated behind a small table. Next to him sat his assistant, who also happened to be his top booker. Composites from the models Franco had already interviewed were off to the side of the table, stacked in two neat piles—one for potential candidates and one for models who didn't make the cut.

"And your name is?" Franco asked in English, his Italian accent noticeable.

"I'm Anna. Anna McKenna."

"A pleasure to meet you, Anna McKenna," Franco said. "This is my assistant, Dawn White."

"Nice to meet you," Anna said to Dawn.

"Likewise," Dawn said flatly, her accent much less noticeable. She put her head down and scanned the list of models she held, checking off Anna's name.

"Have a seat," Franco said.

"Thank you." Anna handed him her portfolio and sat down.

Minutes passed as Franco and Dawn looked through her pictures and sized her up physically. Even though Anna was a bit clumsy, Franco thought she was stunning. Besides, he loved gorgeous redheads, and they were few and far between.

"I like your look," he said, reaching the end of her portfolio.

"Thank you." Intimidated and uncomfortable from being so indiscreetly sized up, Anna did her best to appear confident and composed.

Franco skimmed through her portfolio pictures once again and took out one of her composites. Glancing over the pictures on the front and back, he then checked her statistics.

"She'll work," he said to Dawn, handing her Anna's composite.

"I agree, she's—"

"Would you like to work in Milan for a few months?" he asked Anna, cutting Dawn off mid-sentence.

"For *Amica* and *Donna* magazines?" she blurted out.

"Perhaps," Franco said, closing her portfolio as he leaned back in his chair and gazed unflinchingly into her eyes.

"That would be a fantastic opportunity. I speak Italian, too."

"You do?" His interest in her was now solidified. "You must come then."

"Right away?"

"It's January 9th. The fashion world will pick up in a few weeks, so the sooner the better."

He stood up and handed her back her portfolio. Anna followed suit, but Dawn stayed seated and began looking through composites, embarrassed and hostile because Franco considered her little more than a goffer.

"I'll have to talk it over with my family first," Anna said, knowing they would almost certainly be against the idea of letting her go work in Italy. Just the same, it was exciting, even if it was only a dream.

"Make sure you do," he said slyly, taking hold of her upper arms and kissing her on each cheek. "Goodbye, Anna."

"Thank you. It was a pleasure to meet you, and you too, Ms. White," Anna said.

Dawn looked up at Anna and sneered, unable to hide her secret distaste and bitterness toward models and their undeserved luck.

Yikes. Why is she giving me such a dirty look? Anna thought, smiling awkwardly in an attempt to hide her nerves. She picked up her shoulder bag and portfolio and headed toward the door.

"Anna?" Franco said.

Anna stopped and turned back to Franco.

"Don't forget to tell your family that I can make you a star."

CHAPTER 12

THE PARTY

Mickey finished up work, showered, and drove to New York City to accompany Anna to her agency's anniversary party at Studio 54. Traffic was light heading into the city. He picked up Anna, who was decked out in new gold and black ankle boots, a gold-trimmed black dress, and a black little chubby coat. Mickey was sporting flared beige trousers, a polyester beige and white patterned shirt, and a forest-green leather jacket. They sat excitedly together as Mickey drove his prized possession, the used 1970 green Corvette he managed to buy wholesale from a car auction, through the maze of New York City's hectic traffic toward Studio 54.

"Thanks for taking me to this party," Anna said.

"Anything for my little niece."

"I didn't really want to go, but it's important for business. Natasha insisted that all of her models come. Anyway, I want you to meet someone."

"You do?"

"Well, you don't have a girlfriend and all," Anna said teasingly.

"How do you know I don't have a girlfriend?"

"Well, do you?"

"No."

"OK then."

"Whatever. Anyway, to tell ya the truth, I'm curious about the one and only Studio 54. More importantly though, I don't really want you going on your own. I know you're a grown woman and all, but—"

"I am a grown woman, you're right. That's why I also want to go model in Milan," Anna blurted out.

"Milan? As in Italy?"

They were now stuck in a traffic jam several blocks away from the eponymous disco on West 54th street. Even though it was late, horns were blasting and traffic was at a standstill. No doubt it was due to the frenzy of people blocking the street while trying to get entrance into the internationally famous nightclub.

"Yes, Italy. People in the modeling business say Italy is the place to get beautiful pictures for your portfolio and help make a model a star."

"A star? Hmmm. So when did this happen? Where did this idea even come from?"

"Today at the agency. I had an audition with an agent from Italy and he asked me to go model there. He's here in America scouting for new faces."

"New faces?"

"New models to bring to Italy to model for magazines like *Amica* and *Donna*. You know, the magazines Nonna's sister sends her from Italy. They even have *Italian Vogue* there, and it's full of beautiful pictures of models from all over the world. The quality and creativity are incredible."

Mickey's green Corvette finally reached the front of the parking garage near Studio 54. "I think it's best to park here," Mickey said as he turned in, took a ticket and started driving down the spiral entryway into the lower level.

"So what do you think, Uncle Mickey?"

"I think no. Anyway, your grandma and grandpa would probably never allow you to go."

"I figured you'd say that. Look though, it's not like I would go and be completely lost. I speak Italian after all."

Mickey pulled the car into a cramped parking spot and the two concentrated on getting out. Mickey locked the doors and took hold of Anna's elbow to escort her out of the garage.

"Anna, this idea is a bit much for me to handle right now. Let's concentrate on one thing at a time."

The two made their way up the stairs and out of the garage, turning toward the building with the huge black marque displaying the number 54 in art deco letters. Dumbfounded by the frenzy that lay ahead, they walked toward the throng of fashionably dressed men and women until they reached the boisterous crowd, who were prevented by the now famous red ropes from entering the disco.

"This is crazy," Anna said to Mickey as they reached the crowd and tried to make their way through the eclectic mix of people posing, shouting and raising their hands in order to draw attention to themselves in the hopes of convincing the bouncers—one of which was standing intimidatingly on a cement block in front of the entryway so he could see above the crowd—that they were worthy of the right to gain entrance into the most exclusive nightclub in the world.

"You two!" the bouncer perched on the cement block shouted as he pointed a finger at Anna and Mickey. Granted enormous power, he had the sole task of deciding who could enter the disco because they belonged to the 'it' crowd and who was destined to simply be a wannabe. It was a flagrant display of decadence, exclusion and outright snobbism.

"Does he mean us?" Anna asked Mickey.

But before she and her attractive uncle could even think about the situation, the envious, longing crowd separated and made room for them, the chosen ones, to walk past the red ropes and into the famous nightclub.

"Oh my gosh," Anna muttered discreetly to her uncle. "I can't believe what just happened."

They made their way through the long, dark hallway sloping downward toward the entrance and into the massive 10,000-square-foot disco. The two stopped and gazed openmouthed at the enormous space that lay before them.

"Far out," Mickey eventually managed to say.

"This place is huge," Anna said.

"You got that right." Mickey glanced up at the eighty-foot ceilings and over to the dance floor filled with masses of people gyrating to the song "YMCA" blasting over the sound system. He stared in disbelief at the homosexual men sporting the newest naked look of black leather cop hats and G-strings dancing feverishly on podiums, and the sexily clad women twirling seductively around chase poles—all under a large crescent moon and moving coke spoon. "Far out," Mickey said once again as he peered out over the crowd of outrageously clad men and women.

"This is unbelievable," Anna said as she and Mickey turned to look over at the large circular bar to their right filled with people—renowned or simply beautiful—chitchatting away with drinks in hand. Most of the women hanging around the bar were decked out in the latest fashions, but a few had decided to express their alter ego; one even deciding to skip clothes entirely and wear a corset, without underwear or a bra. Many of the men, clad in the latest male fashion, stood around the bar coolly, but some, transvestites for sure, sashayed about in outrageously flamboyant dresses, playing the part of women they so desperately wanted to be, and even using the women's bathroom when nature called. No one looked twice, or at least pretended not to. This was the late seventies after all, a time of decadence filled with an 'anything goes' mentality.

"Zio, look, there's Truman Capote," Anna said, nudging her uncle.

"Truman Capote? Who's Truman Capote?"

"Zio, he's a famous writer."

"Writer? Anna, I don't read what you read. I only read crime."

"Duh! *In Cold Blood.*"

"*In Cold Blood?* No kiddin'," Mickey said as he scrutinized the man dressed casually in jeans, a tee shirt and fedora hat. "He wrote that?"

"Yes, Zio, he wrote that."

Mickey continued scrutinizing Capote. "He dresses a bit strange for my taste, wearing a flowered scarf and dark sunglasses. What does he need sunglasses for in a place like this?"

"Zio, it's the style. It's cool."

"Guess I'm not cool. And look who he's talkin' to."

"Who's he talking to?"

"Liza Minelli."

"Who's she?"

"Duh." Mickey smiled at Anna and started singing the theme song from Marin Scorsese's hit film *New York, New York.*

"Got me," Anna said affectionately. "Look, I see our group," she said as she spotted Natasha at the far end of the circular bar amongst a group of fashion designers, agents, photographers, art directors, and models—all dressed to the nines and mingling together. "Let's go over there." She grabbed Mickey's hand and led the way over to the group and introduced him to everyone she knew, including Petra, who was making her way toward the dance floor in a silver mini dress while singing and dancing to the tail end of "We Are Family" by Sister Sledge. Mickey ordered himself a beer and a Diet Pepsi for Anna and the two, now comfortably ensconced amongst the fashionable crowd, finally had a chance to speak.

"So, what do you think of Petra?" Anna asked Mickey over the disco music blaring in the background.

"She's a bit wild for me," he said emphatically into Anna's ear while checking out the beautiful Swedish model seductively gyrating to the latest disco song blasting over the sound system.

"She's dying to go out with you."

Hearing only half of what Anna said, Mickey turned serious. "She's dying?"

"No, silly, she's dying to go out with you!"

"Oh, got it. Not my type really."

"Too bad. She's going to be very disappointed. She's the girl I wanted you to meet," Anna said.

"Anna! Anna!" A male voice was calling her name.

Anna turned and spotted Richie Rubin, drink in hand, making his way over to her.

"Oh no, here comes that sleazy photographer I told you about," Anna said under her breath.

"This is the guy?" Now on guard, Mickey straightened up and puffed out his chest. It seemed to be the natural reaction he had when he spotted an uncomfortable or dangerous situation.

Anna knew the reaction well and giggled to herself. "Calm down. He's harmless," she said.

"Hey, babe, how ya doin'?" Richie leaned over to kiss Anna on her cheek and reached out to shake Mickey's hand.

Anna politely introduced the two men. "Richie, this is Mickey Gallo."

"Nice to meet ya," Richie said with a slight smirk. "You a photographer?"

"Nope. I'm a cop," Mickey said flatly.

"Oh, right." Richie froze up with discomfort, stumbled for something to say, and suddenly pretended to spot someone he knew on the other side of their group. "Hey, there's someone I really need to speak to. Catch ya later." He was off in a flash.

"He couldn't wait to get away from you," Anna said, laughing hysterically.

"Yeah, I have that effect on people."

"That was hilarious." Anna noticed Gianni and Jenny, who had just arrived, standing amongst the large group.

"Let's say hello to Gianni and Jenny Gavazzi," Anna said. "You remember them, right?" She led the way toward her favorite photographer and makeup artist.

"Hey, Anna, so good to see you," Jenny said.

"Anna, you look stunning tonight. I need to photograph you in that dress," Gianni said.

"Let's do it. By the way, do you remember my Uncle Mickey?"

"How could we forget?" Jenny and Gianni started laughing. They continued chatting, and before long the small group expanded while people came to say hello and then moved on to get a drink, dance a bit or head over to the bathrooms.

"Hello, Anna."

Surprised, Anna turned to see Franco Rubelli standing right behind her.

"Oh, hi. Franco, right? I met you at Top Form earlier today, didn't I?" Anna knew perfectly well where they met. But she wanted to remain calm and collected, so pretended not to be totally excited at the possibility of going to work in Italy, home to a host of her relatives and a place where she could practice the second language she started learning the day she was born. Just as she was about to introduce Franco to her Uncle Mickey, Paul, the model Anna met at

Top Form, joined the group and the conversation turned to working in Italy.

"I would love to go to work in Milan, but I don't think I'll get the OK from my family," Anna said, looking straight into Mickey's eyes with a twinkle.

Before Mickey could respond, Paul chimed in.

"You want to go too? So do I. Straightaway in fact. It would be great if we could go together."

"Yes, Anna, you should definitely come," Franco said, now on a mission to persuade Anna to come work in Milan. He was convinced more than ever that she had what it took to make it big in Italy. Besides, he loved redheads.

The group continued talking about the business and modeling in Italy while Mickey went to get another beer. Suddenly they were interrupted by an obviously intoxicated Petra.

"Anna, I'm not feeling very well," Petra said, slurring her words. Clearly drunk, she hung on to Anna for fear of falling over.

"Oh no. Do you want to go home?"

"Yeeees, but I can't find my handbag."

"Really? Did you check everywhere?"

"Uh huh. But maybe I didn't bring it," Petra said, holding her queasy stomach.

"OK, perhaps it will show up later. What color is it?"

"My favorite color. Red!"

"OK, let's get you in a cab now." Anna turned to look for her uncle, who was heading back to the group with a beer in tow.

"Petra isn't feeling well and wants to go home," Anna said to Mickey. The two of them agreed it was best to get Petra into a taxi, but not before Anna took a quick look around for the missing handbag while Mickey propped up the teetering young model.

"No luck. I hope no one stole it," Anna said.

"If they did, it's too late now," Mickey said. "It'll be long gone. At least the money will. The bag may show up in a garbage can later."

"That makes sense," Anna said.

"Let's get her in a taxi." Mickey held one of Petra's arms while Anna did the same with the other. They led the poor girl out of the disco and up through the long tunnel-like hallway.

"You had a coat, right?" Anna asked.

"Uh huh," Petra said, exaggeratedly nodding her head up and down.

"Do you have a coat check ticket?" Mickey asked.

Petra fumbled past her silver dress into her bra and managed to pull out the now sweat-infused small piece of crumpled paper with the number 68 on it.

"Here it is," she said proudly as she continued teetering to and fro on her high heels.

"Hang on to her while I go get her coat," Mickey said, taking the ticket and heading over to the coat check. He quickly returned with a bright red coat and both Anna and Mickey helped Petra get into it.

"And your keys?" Mickey asked.

"Keys? Keys!" Petra exclaimed, sloppily pulling a set out of her coat pocket and holding them proudly up for Mickey and Anna to see.

Anna took the keys from Petra before she dropped them and put them back into Petra's coat pocket.

"OK, Petra, let's get you in a taxi now," Mickey said.

They escorted the young blonde out the door into the late night air, where bouncers stood by ready to help departing customers. Quickly summing up the situation, one of the bouncers whistled toward the line of standing taxis eagerly waiting for their chance to take an early morning customer home. A taxi pulled up and the bouncer opened the door of the passenger seat while Mickey and

Anna helped Petra inside. Falling back against the tattered leather seat, Petra looked up at Mickey.

"You're sooooo cute!"

"Your address?" he asked, ignoring Petra's come-on.

"My address. Hmmm. I just moved there. Let me think. Right, right. I remember now. It's 165 Duane Street."

"Manhattan?"

"Yes, Tribeca," Petra said, proud to get the words out of her mouth.

The taxi driver, unfazed by a situation all too common, simply looked back at Mickey and waited for instructions. Mickey pulled out his badge, showed it to the driver and handed him a twenty-dollar bill.

"Get her home safely."

CHAPTER 13

SURPRISE

The doorbell rang, waking Petra from a deep slumber. Still feeling the effects from too much alcohol at the party earlier, she finally managed to look over at the alarm clock.

"Who's here at this hour?" she said to herself when she noticed it was 3:00 a.m. The doorbell rang again, so she groggily forced herself up and made her way into the living room and over to the video screen on the wall next to the entrance door. Peering into the lit screen, she could see the fuzzy outline of a man she recognized. Certain that she knew him from the fashion business, but unable to remember exactly where she had met him, she lifted the receiver and pressed the button.

"Hello?" she asked.

Suddenly a close-up of her handbag covered the whole screen.

"Hey, that's my handbag," she exclaimed.

"That's why I'm here. I found it a little while ago at Studio 54."

"Oh my gosh, I'm so happy!"

"I thought you'd say that."

"Well, come on up. I'm on the third floor." Petra buzzed him in and quickly glanced into the mirror, rubbing her eyes and smoothing her hair. She looked down at her silly pink and green flowered nightgown. *Oh well.* She opened the door, turned on the hall light and leaned back on the doorframe, all the while trying to remember how she knew this man. Suddenly it came to her. "That's who he is," she said aloud moments before the elevator reached her floor, stopped with a thud and opened.

He walked out, dangling the handbag. "Sorry to wake you, but I knew you were looking for this," he said, holding her bag out in front of him as he walked down the corridor toward her.

"Oh that's no problem at all," she said, smiling ear to ear. "Thank you so much for bringing it down here." She looked down momentarily and scratched her head. "I wonder why I couldn't find it."

"I'm sure it was because it was so dark in the disco. I just happened to be standing by the bar and my foot hit it," he said, handing her the bag. "When I looked down I saw a bright red handbag and remembered you had been looking for it."

"Well, I'm thrilled," she said, not wanting to ask more because of embarrassment from her drunken behavior earlier. "Come in, please," she said, holding the open door.

"Are you sure? It's late."

"Absolutely. You came all the way down here for me," she said, plopping the handbag on the entrance console.

"Just for a minute then."

"Let me take your coat," she said.

He took off his gloves and put them in his pocket before handing it to her.

"Would you like a glass of Coca Cola or a cup of coffee?" she asked, unaware of his intense gaze as she hung the coat on a set of hooks near the door. "Unfortunately that's all we have because we just moved in," she continued as she turned and bent down, reaching for the lower shelf of the entrance table and switching on her stereo.

"We? You live with someone?" he asked, leering at her body, now transparent under the floor light shining directly onto her thin cotton nightgown.

"Yes, Anika. But she's not here at the moment; she's still in Holland," she said, standing up and moving away from the floor lamp and back toward the sofa.

"Coffee or Coke?" she asked him. "I mean the liquid variety of course," she continued playfully.

"A Coca Cola would be nice, thank you."

"Great. Have a seat. I'll be back in a minute." Petra motioned to a long, wooden-framed, beige sofa while heading to the kitchen, still unaware of his leering eyes following her every movement. Once in the kitchen, she took out a bottle of Coca Cola from the refrigerator and poured it into two tall glasses, all the while thinking about how lucky she and Anika were to have found this brand-new conversion. Even if Tribeca was still relatively uninhabited it was worth it simply because their apartment was so large in comparison to all the other cookie-cutters dotting New York City.

She took a small bowl, filled it with potato chips and put everything neatly on a tray. Smiling happily to herself while she thought about all the wonderful parties she and Anika would have one day soon, she walked back into the living room.

"This is a strange area for you two to live in. There's no one around this part of the city," he said as she placed the tray on the coffee table.

"I know, just a few artists here and there. But look at this living room. It's huge!" she said enthusiastically.

"True."

"So are our bedrooms and bathrooms. Would you like to see?" she asked naively.

"No that's OK, I believe you," he said flatly.

"Where are my cigarettes?" she suddenly wondered aloud. She stooped and looked through the papers scattered on the coffee table but found none.

"Sorry, but I don't have any, otherwise I'd offer you one," he said.

"Oh don't worry, I must have a pack somewhere." Petra stood back up, walked over to the entry table and opened her handbag. Scouring through it, she eventually pulled out an empty pack. "Darn!" She walked across the living room to her darkened bedroom. "Excuse me one minute."

Now that she couldn't find a cigarette, she wanted one desperately. With her back turned to the bedroom door, she hovered over her dimly lit nightstand drawer and began frantically rummaging through the mess, unaware that he had quietly snuck up behind her. *Damn*, she thought, *how can I not have a single cigarette?* Dismayed and realizing that she wasn't going to be able to quench her unrelenting desire for a cigarette, she gave up, closed the drawer and turned back toward the living room. And right into his grasp.

In one swift motion, he grabbed her and threw her down on the bed.

Alarmed, she was unable to uncomprehend what was going on.

"Cockteaser," he said viciously as he wrestled her down on the bed.

Completely shocked and dazed, Petra tried to speak, but only managed to sputter incoherently while squirming with all of her strength in a desperate effort to get up.

"Bitch!" he seethed through clenched teeth. In one quick feral move, he straddled the top of her hips, pinning her body down against the mattress. The terror in Petra's eyes only heightened his savage desire. He slammed the back of her head into the pillow and began smothering her nose and mouth with an open palm. Frozen with fear, Petra was unable to move under his muscular frame and the brute strength of his outstretched hand.

"I'll show you," he growled. Now a ferocious animal with monstrous eyes, any semblance of the charming man he was had vanished.

"Stop! Stop! Please!" Whimpering and petrified, she was defenseless under his hulking body.

"I'm going to give you what you deserve, you stupid bitch!" Seething, he undid his trousers and pulled out his cock.

Petrified for her life, she no longer fought back, lying lifelessly as he thrust himself inside her.

"Slut!"

"Please don't," she whimpered helplessly.

"This'll teach you, you cockteaser." He continued thrusting until he climaxed, groaning with satisfaction. After a few seconds he got off the bed. Calmly, he zipped up his trousers. "You let me up here. You know you wanted this."

Petra was in a state of shock, unable to speak.

He looked at her contemptuously as he put on his coat and gloves, muttering under his breath, possessed with anger once again.

When dawn rose over the city several hours later, sunlight streaming through the third-floor bedroom window illuminated a gruesome scene—Petra sprawled on her bed, her throat slit from ear to ear, the last remnants of her life drained away.

⅄

"Top Form," Jo Ellen said as she answered the phone in a cheerful voice. The phones were ringing off the hook as the bookers, seated around the large round table, expertly dealt with the influx. Now that the holidays were behind them and 1979 had officially started, the fashion world was up and running again.

"Yes, could I speak with Jo Ellen?"

"This is she, how can I help you?"

"Jo Ellen, this is Amy from Harry Biggin's studio."

"What can I do for you, Amy?" Jo Ellen racked her brain to remember details about why Amy might be calling.

"Petra was supposed to be at the studio at 8:30 this morning, but she still hasn't shown up."

Jo Ellen, now remembering this booking for Petra, looked up at the white clock on the wall displaying 9:30 a.m. in big, bold numbers.

"Oh dear. I am so sorry. She must have overslept. I'll call her immediately and get right back to you." Jo Ellen hung up and reached for Petra's agenda card from the revolving center tabletop files. Spotting Petra's personal information listed at the top, Jo Ellen dialed Petra's number. The phone started ringing, and as she waited she looked at the details of the booking.

"I'm sure I gave her the right starting time," she mumbled to herself as the phone continued to ring. No one answered. Strange, she thought as she redialed the number. It doesn't make sense; the studio is just a few blocks away from where she lives. Jo Ellen hung up and walked over to Natasha's office and knocked on her door.

"Come in."

Jo Ellen opened the door to the elegant white office to find Natasha, chic as ever in black palazzo pants and coordinating turtleneck, covering the mouthpiece to the telephone and motioning for Jo Ellen to sit down.

"OK, Franco, I'll work on getting Anna and Petra over to Milan in a few weeks. Have a safe flight back. Ciao, ciao." Natasha hung up. "What's up?" she asked Jo Ellen.

"Petra hasn't shown up for her booking. She was supposed to be there at 8:30," Jo Ellen said, concern on her face.

"Naturally you've tried calling her?"

"Many times. She's not answering her phone."

"Maybe she's stuck in the subway or something."

"That's what I thought, but the studio is only a few blocks from her home."

"Hmmm. Well, it wouldn't be the first time this has happened with one of our models. Call around to some of the girls she's close to. Maybe they know where she is."

"Right. Will do."

"Who's the client?"

"Isabella Designs. They're shooting the summer catalogue at Harry Biggin's studio down in Tribeca."

"OK, I'll call over there right away. We need to apologize and see if there's another model they might like who can replace Petra at the last minute. God knows how much the shooting cost to arrange. Between the photographer, makeup artist, hair stylist and other models' fees, it's a fortune I'm sure."

Jo Ellen left Natasha's office and started calling around to Petra's friends. She couldn't get ahold of most of them because they were either working or out on auditions, so she was left asking the girls about Petra as they called to check in throughout the day for their schedule updates. Unfortunately, no one had seen Petra the entire weekend. Around 4 p.m. Jo Ellen dialed Petra one more time, but she still didn't answer, so she headed back into Natasha's office.

"There's still no answer. I've also spoken to some of her friends and the last time they saw her was at our anniversary party at Studio 54."

"Oh. How strange," Natasha said as a sinking feeling grabbed the pit of her stomach.

"I know. What do you think we should do?" Jo Ellen asked, now white as a ghost.

"Well, I think we need to call the police, don't you?" Natasha stared steadily at Jo Ellen, both knowing what the other one was thinking, and dialed 911.

One ring later a woman answered the phone. "What's your emergency please?"

Natasha continued staring at Jo Ellen with dread in her eyes. "I'd like to report a missing person."

⋏

Detective Tansey reached a grid of streets down in Tribeca and continued driving through the mostly desolate neighborhood lined with predominantly empty commercial buildings. He was looking for one of the few recent building conversions, which had sprung up in the form of new lofts due to a sudden desirability to live in the area by artists, photographers and people in the creative industries craving big loft space. Reaching the newly converted building on Duane Street, he spotted Ramsey and Moran, the officers who had called him to the crime scene. He parked his car and got out. After a quick hello, they headed into the building and took the elevator to the third floor. The death of a young woman was always a sad occasion, and although weathered by years of police work, the officers couldn't help but feel saddened and reticent, particularly when the victim was murdered so gruesomely. Once the elevator doors opened on the third floor, the team headed down toward the cordoned off door where Officers Herkel, Smith and Kasinski from the crime lab stood by.

"Prepare yourself," Ramsey said as he opened the door to Petra's apartment.

Walking in, they were accosted by a fetid smell of decay. No one spoke as they made their way to the bedroom, where Petra was sprawled out dead in her bed with her throat slit and a pool of black, mostly dried blood puddled on the floor beside her. Detective Tansey glanced around for a few moments.

"How long do you suppose she's been lying here?" Moran asked.

"Hard to tell," Tansey answered

"I'd say several days judging by the smell and the color of her skin," Herkel added.

"This is just like the murder that happened nine months ago over in the Meatpacking District," Ramsey said.

"Yep, another model with a slit throat. Think we're dealing with a serial killer?" Moran asked.

"Who knows. Could be a jilted lover or someone with a nasty grudge," Tansey said.

"Best not to assume anything at this stage," Ramsey said.

"I agree with that," Kasinski added while putting on gloves.

"What do ya say we get started," Tansey said.

"Right. The sooner we get done, the sooner we can get this poor girl out of here," Moran said.

Smith inspected the door and then headed over to the windows. "Doesn't look like a forced entry. She must have known her killer."

"You would think so, unless the perp convinced her to let him up for some reason," Tansey said.

Tansey and Herkel began looking in detail at Petra and the surrounding mattress.

"Looks like she's been raped," Herkel said.

Tansey took a look at Petra's legs and noticed bruises and signs of trauma. He shook his head in dismay.

"Over here, guys. Look," Kasinski said, pointing to the floor on the side of the bed opposite the pooled blood.

The group of officers walked over to Kasinski.

"Looks like the perp left a handkerchief," Kasinski said as he clicked away with his camera.

Several photos later, Smith picked up the handkerchief, ready to put it in an evidence bag. "This is definitely going to be—wait, what's that smell?"

"On the handkerchief?" Tansey asked.

"Yeah. I recognize it," Smith said. "It's a spice or something. Can't place it though."

Smith held the handkerchief under Tansey's nose while the rest of the men gathered round.

"I don't smell anything," Herkel said.

"Me neither, but I have allergies. I can't smell very well," Moran added.

"I definitely smell something," Tansey said. "I don't know what it is, but we need to check it out."

Smith dropped the handkerchief into the evidence bag and Kasinski resumed taking photos elsewhere while the other officers continued looking for evidence. Every nook and cranny was searched for fingerprints and hair. Several hours later all possible clues had been collected and the team was ready to move on.

"Let's call the coroner's office," Tansey said to the group of exhausted men. "It's time we get this poor girl outta here."

The weary men let out a sigh of relief. It had been a tough day, one they hoped never to relive again anytime soon.

"So you went to your anniversary party at Studio 54 and that's the last time you saw her."

"Yes, that's the last time," Natasha said, a flood of tears springing from her eyes. She couldn't believe that the same thing had happened yet again to another one of her models. "Do you think Rhonda's murder is connected to this one?" she asked Detective Tansey from behind her white Chippendale desk.

Tansey scribbled a few notes and then handed Natasha a tissue from the antique gold tissue box on Natasha's desk. He felt bad; it was the second time she had to deal with such a tragedy, but that was life ... especially in NYC.

"Could be, but it also could just be a coincidence. I hate to say it, but it's an easy way to kill someone, especially if you have a deep-seated hatred of the person. Unfortunately, young women are easy targets. Anyway, why don't you tell me about her."

"Well, she was a very sweet girl. Everyone loved her. She could be a bit too friendly though. Naive really."

"You saying she was the type who could have let the killer in, even if she didn't know him well?"

"It would be like her. She could be far too trusting."

"Do you know who she was she talking to at the party?"

"Everyone really. We were a big crowd. Everyone was mingling and dancing." Natasha momentarily stopped crying as she remembered the great time everyone had at Studio 54.

"And your guest list, who was on it?"

"All the important fashion people," she said proudly.

"Fashion people?" Tansey had never heard that term before.

"Excuse me, I'm just referring to people like photographers, advertising agents, art directors, fashion editors, designers ... the list goes on and on."

"I see. Can you give me some names?"

"Let's see. Well, there were lots of models of course, and then several photographers—"

"Like who specifically?" he said, gently trying to prod her for more information.

"Well, Gianni Gavazzi was there, but he was with his wife."

"Unfortunately that doesn't mean anything. Married men have been known to kill," Tansey said. He had been a detective for years and had seen everything, learning a long time ago that one could never really tell who was living a double life. "Who else can you think of?" Tansey asked, scribbling Gianni Gavazzi's name in his tattered notebook.

"There was Richie Rubin, Harry Biggin, Jean Luc Rene, Peter Birk, Silvia Paran. The list is long. All of our best clients were invited, including clients from out of town—even out of the country for that matter."

Realizing how long the list was about to be, he put his pen and notebook back in the pocket of his blazer. "We're going to need the names of everyone on your guest list. I'll need their phone numbers and addresses too. They're all going to need to give us their alibis."

"Everyone? Including women?"

"Everyone."

"Hmm, you think a woman could have done this?" Natasha's eyes opened wide.

"No. The victim was raped, but a woman might know something. She might even be an accomplice. We can never rule that out."

"Huh, I never thought about that. Anyway, as you said, the murderer may not be anyone in the fashion business. At least I hope not," Natasha said.

"At this point we don't know, so, as I mentioned, I'll need the names and contact information of all of your guests that night."

"Certainly, detective. I'll have my secretary give it to you before you leave. The thing is, so many of the people in our business travel a lot. I just hope you can find them."

"Let us worry about that. By the way, did the deceased have a boyfriend?"

"No, I don't think so. She was due to meet someone that night at the party, someone she was interested in."

Tansey's ears perked up as he pulled out his pen and notebook once again. Maybe this will lead us somewhere, he thought. "Oh, who would that be?"

"Well, he's our model Anna's uncle."

Tansey made a quick note in his notebook. "Sounds like he would be a good guy to start with."

"Detective, I'm sure he has nothing to do with it. He's a detective, just like you."

"A detective, huh?" Tansey said, nodding while thinking about the crazy headline that would make: Detective Killer on the Loose.

CHAPTER 14

No Way

"Thanks, but I know where his office is," Mickey said to the police officer stationed at the front desk. He led Anna down the brightly lit, shabby hallway's cheap linoleum floor and knocked on the door.

"Come in."

"Hi there," Mickey said, opening the door and allowing Anna to enter first.

Tansey stood up abruptly, almost knocking over his desk. Although he knew a model was coming to his office to be questioned, he'd been too busy to ponder the reality of that fact. Usually confronted with the dregs of society, he was totally unprepared to greet one of the most beautiful women he had ever seen in his life.

"Detective Tansey, this is Anna McKenna. Anna, Detective Tansey."

Regaining his composure, Tansey reached out and shook both Anna's and Mickey's hands.

"Please, have a seat," he said, gesturing to the two chairs in front of his desk. Slightly embarrassed by his small, dismal office featuring nothing but a plaque he received awhile back, he quickly took out his pack of cigarettes and offered one to Anna.

"Oh, thank you," Anna said, taking one out of the pack.

Mickey turned to look at Anna. "When did you start smoking?"

"Recently," she said, noting Mickey's displeasure with this new information. "But I only smoke when I'm nervous. A lot of models do." Anna leaned in toward Tansey, allowing the detective to light it for her.

"You have nothing to be nervous about, Anna. This is standard investigation stuff," Mickey said, unaware that he was actually a suspect.

Tansey took a drag on his cigarette and then looked from Mickey to Anna. He could tell that Mickey was completely at ease, but Anna was obviously very uncomfortable and distressed. He felt bad having to call them both into his office, but he had to get the story straight. Unfortunately, her uncle may have something to hide and he wanted to get to the bottom of it all as quickly as possible, before there was another murder.

"Gallo, I know you're a detective and all, but I gotta ask you, did you have a thing going on with the deceased?"

Anna answered before Mickey could say a word. "No, no he didn't. Petra was hoping that might happen, but—"

"I see. So exactly when did you first meet Petra?" Tansey asked Mickey.

Again, Anna blurted out a response, not giving her uncle the opportunity to answer. "At Top Form's anniversary party. Petra asked me to bring my uncle there because she desperately wanted to meet him."

"So you first met her that night?" Tansey asked Mickey.

"Yeah, that night," Mickey said, realizing what this meeting at Tansey's office was all about. He was being interrogated; he was a suspect.

"But my uncle didn't like her. He thought she was too wild."

"Let me get this straight. You met her at the party, didn't like her, and then what?"

"She got a little drunk and was feeling sick, so we ended up putting her in a taxi and sending her home," Mickey said, slightly annoyed.

"Intoxicated … mmm. Anything else?" Tansey asked.

Anna and Mickey took a minute to think about what had happened.

"It was a bad ending to a really good night. Everyone was having a great time, including Petra, but she clearly didn't pay attention to how much alcohol she was consuming," Anna said. "And she probably didn't eat much either."

"What Anna says is true. It was a bad ending to a really good night."

"Hey, I remember something though," Anna blurted out. "She couldn't find her handbag."

"That's right," Mickey said. "Then she said she couldn't even remember if she had brought it."

Tansey thought a minute about a red handbag the officers noticed on the entry table at the crime scene.

"Was it red?" Tansey asked.

"Yes, how'd you know?" Anna said.

"It's his job to know," Mickey said.

"Exactly," Tansey said. He made a mental note to have it dusted for fingerprints. "Go on."

"I figured if she had brought one and couldn't find it, it was probably either stolen and long gone, or anywhere given the crowd at the enormous disco and her condition. I thought it was best to get her in a taxi and send her home."

"What about her keys? How was she going to get in her apartment?"

"She had them in her coat pocket, so I knew she could get in," Mickey said.

Tansey looked sympathetically at Anna, teary eyed by now, and then back over to Mickey.

Mickey stared unblinkingly at Tansey. He knew what was going on—Tansey wanted more information. "We put her in the taxi, I gave the driver a twenty, showed him my badge, and told him to get her home safely."

"Did you get the medallion number?"

Mickey pulled out a piece of paper containing the medallion number and the driver's name. Tansey took the paper and looked at Mickey. *Good cop,* he thought.

"That was it, Detective Tansey," Anna said as she wiped her eyes with a tissue.

Tansey took a moment to digest this information then looked at Anna and Mickey. "Did you go back to the party?"

"No, we decided to leave. I drove Anna out to her grandparents—my parents—so she could spend the weekend visiting with them and her little brother, Joey. They all live in Port Chester."

"Were they home?"

"Yeah, fast asleep, but they got up for us," Mickey said.

"My grandmother made us some chamomile tea and gave us some of her homemade pound cake. Then my grandfather joined us. Both of them were so excited to hear about the party at Studio 54," Anna said as she nervously snuffed out her cigarette butt. She was beginning to realize that her uncle was actually a suspect.

"Right. OK. So, you chitchatted for a while. Then what did you do?" Tansey asked, looking directly at Mickey.

"As Anna said, we sat around talking. In fact, Anna brought up this idea about modeling in Italy."

"Italy?"

"Yeah, seems to be a common thing," Mickey said.

"It's true, detective. Models from America go to Milan, Paris, even Tokyo, to work. Petra and I both wanted to go to Milan," Anna said.

"Milan?"

"Milan, Italy. We met the agent from Italy earlier that day at Top Form. He was in New York scouting for models who could potentially work there."

"I see," Tansey said, not knowing anything about the modeling world or its inner workings. "Who is this agent?"

"His name is Franco Rubelli," Anna said.

"And he lives in Italy?"

"Yes, he does."

"I see. And you wanted to go to model there?" Tansey asked, taking notes to investigate Rubelli.

"Absolutely," Anna said, forgetting momentarily about why she and her uncle were sitting in Detective Tansey's office.

Mickey sensed Tansey's bewilderment. "At first I was against the whole thing, but my parents are from Italy so it seemed like an interesting idea—Anna could practice her Italian and get to know her heritage," Mickey said. "Anyway, after a while I got tired and crashed on their couch for a few hours. Anna, you went to sleep in your old bedroom, right?"

"Right, but first my little brother, Joey, woke up and came downstairs. I guess he overheard us talking. Anyway, he was hungry 'cause it was already 5:30 in the morning, so my grandma didn't go to sleep. She stayed up," Anna said.

"That was it. Then I went home, showered and went to work." Mickey was perturbed by now. "You think I'm a suspect, don't you?"

Horrified at hearing it said so bluntly, Anna started sobbing uncontrollably. "My uncle was with me. He's not a murderer!"

"I know, I know. You're off the hook, Gallo. But tell me, Miss McKenna, can you think of anyone that could have done this? Anyone at all. Doesn't have to be someone from the party."

Anna took a deep breath, relieved by Tansey's words. "Well, I did meet someone I didn't like when I was in line waiting to pay at Bloomingdale's. Petra said she'd met him before, too."

"Who was that?" Mickey asked. First taken aback by Anna's smoking, he was even more unnerved by this new information.

She sighed. "This man named Alex Findler. He claimed to be a movie producer and insisted he could make me a star."

"Why didn't you tell me about this guy?"

"I didn't want to worry you. Anyway, I got rid of him."

"What do you mean, you got rid of him?" Tansey asked.

"I just mean I got away from him."

"And Petra knew him?" Mickey asked, now acting like the detective he was.

"She had a similar experience with him. He walked her home once and tried to convince her to come to his studio for a screen test."

"He knew where she lived?" Tansey asked.

"Oh no, not where she lived in Tribeca. This is when she was living with us at Natasha's," Anna said.

"I see. Did he give you his number?" Tansey asked

"Right, did he give you his number?" Mickey asked, looking from Tansey over to Anna. He was in full detective mode now, determined to catch this murderer.

"Yes, I have his business card somewhere."

"I need to see that," Tansey and Mickey said simultaneously. They looked at each other with confusion, as it was now unclear as to who was doing the interview.

Mickey shut up, realizing he was overstepping his boundaries.

"Miss McKenna, can you think of any other suspicious men, men you don't like, men who have bad habits, shall we say."

Anna sat for a bit before she spoke up. She didn't want to get anyone in trouble, but on the other hand, her friend was brutally murdered. Finally she spoke up. "I don't like the photographer Richie Rubin much."

"How do you know him?" Tansey asked.

Before Anna could answer, Mickey questioned her. "Is that the guy you introduced me to?"

"Right, him."

"Why don't you like him, Miss McKenna?" Tansey continued.

"He's sleazy. He's got a reputation for touching the models in inappropriate ways. Also, he's always drinking and doing a lot of cocaine. In fact, he wants anyone who's working for him to party along, even on the job."

Mickey was dismayed by this information. He trusted Anna when she said there were a lot of good people in her business, but he hated thinking about the sleazeballs. He turned from Anna to Tansey. "I could tell he had a lot to hide. I met him that night at Studio, and when I told him I was a cop he took off like a bat out of hell."

"Typical. He could just be seedy, as you say, or maybe he's hiding something. I'll need to bring him in." Tansey looked back at Anna. "Is there anyone else you find to be a little ... sleazy, shall we say?"

"Come to think of it, we did meet this weird guy a while back."

"We?" Tansey said.

"Yes, Anika, Sue, Petra and me."

"Who was he?" Mickey was disgusted. He couldn't believe the amount of creeps Anna had already encountered.

"I think he said his name was Dunbar."

"Don Dunbar?" Tansey looked at Anna, horrified.

"Right. Supposedly, he's the son of the famous photographer Dennis Dunbar. He seemed sleazy though, dirty too. He smelled yucky and his hair was all greasy."

"Fatniski," Tansey muttered.

Mickey was blown away. "You actually met this guy?" Mickey asked, shocked that Anna had already come in contact with so many predators.

"Yeah, at Serendipity. Why?"

"Never mind, Anna. Just tell us how this happened." Mickey, dismay written all over his face, looked over to Tansey.

"Yes. Please continue, Miss McKenna."

"Let me think a moment. Right, now I remember. He spilled his milkshake on Petra's jeans and then, before you know it, he just sat down and started talking to us."

"When was this?" Tansey asked.

"Right before Christmas."

"Did you see him again?" Mickey asked.

"No. No way. Like I said, I thought he was a creep." Anna pondered a moment. "I don't know, there was something odd about him. Sue and Anika didn't like him either, but Petra … she likes everybody. I mean, she liked everybody."

Anna started tearing up again. Tansey handed her another tissue.

"So you don't know if she saw him after that?"

"No, I don't. A few days after we met him, the agency closed down for the holidays and she and Anika moved into their new apartment. I didn't see her again until the party at Studio 54."

The detectives sat in disbelief. They had been convinced Fatniski would make himself scarce.

"Anything else?" Tansey asked.

"Well, Petra wasn't getting as much work as before and she had this crazy idea she was fat. I think she thought this guy could help her somehow. Maybe get her work with his father. Or supposed father."

"I see. Was he at your agency's party?" Tansey asked.

"Yeah, did I meet him?" Mickey was clenching his hands, his anger boiling over.

"No, no, you didn't meet him. He wasn't at the party. Having said that, I suppose he could have been at Studio 54 though, since it was packed. But I didn't see him." Exhausted, Anna put her head in her hands and began sobbing again.

Tansey grabbed another tissue from his drawer and passed it to her. He and Mickey locked eyes, reading each other's minds.

"OK, I think we can wrap this up." As far as Tansey was concerned the interview was over. He knew in his heart Mickey Gallo had nothing to do with the murders, and that Anna had told him everything she knew. "Thanks for your help," he said as he stood up, signaling the end of their meeting.

"No problem at all," Mickey said, relieved that it was over. Anna dried her tears and the two of them stood up and shook Tansey's outstretched hand. "Man, I hope you can get to the bottom of this as soon as possible," Mickey said.

"So do we, Gallo," Detective Tansey said. He looked over to Anna. "Thank you, Miss McKenna. Take care of yourself, will ya."

MILAN, ITALY 1979

CHAPTER 15

FEBRUARY

Franco leaned against the open door of his agency, Franco Rubelli Models, arms crossed in front of his chest and a smirk of satisfaction on his face as he waited to greet his latest arrival from New York City. The power he wielded because of his stature in the European modeling world turned him on—it was an aphrodisiac and he relished in it. He earned a lot of money, so much so that he could rent space to house his agency in a prominent 19th century Italianate limestone building on a prestigious tree-lined piazza in central Milan. It was a long way from the dilapidated shack he grew up in, and a very long way from his abusive mother and ineffectual father, parents he hadn't seen since he left home and went to work at Milan Management, the crème de la crème of modeling agencies, before opening his own.

The elegant antique elevator creaked to a stop and Anna emerged from behind the beautiful black wrought iron gate.

"I've made it," she said, spotting Franco as she maneuvered the two large suitcases she had lugged with her out of the elevator and onto the hallway floor.

"Anna, welcome to Italy." Franco, smiling ear to ear and oozing charm, walked over to Anna and took her suitcases. "Let's leave these here shall we," he said, placing them to the side of the hallway and then glancing back at Anna. "You look splendid, my dear, even after an eight-hour flight."

"Thank you," Anna said, feeling much more exhausted than splendid. Giving no further thought to her luggage, she kissed Franco on each cheek in the customary European fashion.

"You are ravishing as always, Anna, but what is this on your face?" Franco touched her chin and held her face for a moment.

"Huh?" Noticing the mirrored hallway, Anna turned and saw what Franco was talking about. Ivory-colored patch marks of loose blotting powder covered her face, lending a bizarre look to her otherwise perfect makeup application.

"Oh dear," she said, giggling with embarrassment. "I powdered my face without a mirror and this is the result."

Quickly fluffing off the loose powder, she composed herself and turned back to Franco, who was charmed by this young woman. Not only was she beautiful, she appeared to be completely innocent and natural, so unlike many of the overly confident, even arrogant, models he dealt with every day.

"Come with me. Let me introduce you to everyone," he said, flicking a strand of hair off her face and deciding immediately that he had to have her.

"Absolutely. I'm so excited to meet them."

Franco took Anna's hand and first introduced her to a few models lounging on the two sleek black leather sofas, and then to the fashionably dressed receptionist perched behind a small glass and chrome desk. After that, he led her through the double doors separating the reception room from the back office.

Anna, feeling daunted by Franco and his commanding energy, followed along, awestruck as she observed the hallways lined with framed magazine covers featuring many of Franco's models posing for *Italian Vogue, Bazaar, Amica, Donna*, and on and on. The magazine covers and their editorial content were extraordinarily beautiful, something the Italians were known for and the reason why so many models from all over the world hoped to be chosen to come model in Milan.

Turning the corner into the booking room, Franco and Anna were greeted by a gaggle of bookers sitting around a big table filled with charts and telephones. Anna met Cecilia and Francesca, then Franco introduced her to Giacomo, the agency's messenger, who delivered portfolios of Franco Rubelli Models' pictures for viewing to potential clients all over the city. Next, he turned his attention to Dawn, who had just hung up the telephone.

"Anna, remember Dawn? You'll be reporting directly to her. She handles all of our new models in Milan." Turning back to Dawn, he said, "She's beautiful, no?"

"Yes, she's different," Dawn responded. She slowly gave Anna the once-over.

"Are you American?" Anna asked, noticing Dawn spoke English with almost no accent.

"Half American, half Italian," Dawn said flatly, inviting no further conversation.

"I see," was all Anna could muster. Intimidated, she could hardly forget the dirty look Dawn gave her the day they had met at Top Form. Anna wondered if this woman's strange behavior had something to do with her appearance. Not only was Dawn a plain Jane with stringy mousy brown hair, her tiny stature was almost farcical alongside the tall, gorgeous models she managed every day—men and women who were born with the immediate advantage of beauty.

"I have her starting on auditions first thing tomorrow," Dawn said to Franco, speaking as if Anna were invisible. "She also has a fitting scheduled for Federico's show."

"Fantastic," Franco said. He turned his attention to Anna. "Your first week is going to be a little slow, unfortunately. All of the designers finished auditions for Milan Fashion Week last week, but we did manage to get you in with Federico sight unseen."

"Sorry I couldn't get here sooner," Anna said, feeling a little guilty for arriving in Milan a week later than originally planned. "I had a terrible flu and was too sick travel."

"Not to worry, darling," Franco said sympathetically. "You'll be busy soon enough."

"She also has options to work for *Amica* and *Grazia* next week," Dawn said, once again speaking as if Anna wasn't present.

"There you go, Anna," Franco said.

Dawn's phone rang, putting their discussion on hold. A lengthy conversation in Italian ensued between Franco, Dawn, and whoever was on the other end of the phone.

Anna, not wanting to eavesdrop, walked a few feet away. Left alone with her thoughts, it wasn't long before she felt a pang of sadness, first for Petra, and then for leaving her family, particularly Joey. Determined not to let the melancholic thoughts get the best of her, she focused instead on the fact modeling in Italy for a few months would make a dramatic difference in the trajectory of her career and enable her to help her family financially. She was determined more than ever to become super successful in Milan so when she returned to America the beautiful pictures she would take back with her would help her become more famous than ever and make oodles of money. Her mother's last words, "Take care of our family, Anna," were lodged in her mind and her determination to help Joey was stuck solidly in her heart. *Enough,* she thought. *I don't want to think about this anymore.*

She wandered over to an eight by ten foot wall displaying composite cards of the striking models Franco Rubelli's agency represented. Intrigued by the more diverse European style, she noticed how dramatic the makeup and clothing were in the photographs used for the models' composites in comparison to the peaches and cream images so popular in the United States. It was Europe after all, and along with France, Italy was known to be a major center of high fashion. Overflowing with abundant freedom to create, the makeup artists embraced sophisticated effects utilizing the newest makeup techniques, and the hairdressers manipulated the models' hair into the most outrageous creations. Models from Nordic countries were big in Milan, alongside Americans, and the occasional exotic beauty. Glancing down the wall, Anna spotted Paul's chiseled and buff physique staring back at her from a small display of male models' composites separated and off to the side. He looked terrific. She was looking forward to seeing him. He had already been in Milan for a week, so perhaps he could show her around a bit.

"Anna, sorry about that," Franco said as he walked up behind her. "I was just on the phone with a client who was expecting Petra to model for his catalogue. I had to explain the unfortunate situation."

Anna's face fell.

"You knew that Petra was going to come to work in Milan along with you, right?"

"Yes, of course," she said, looking down at the floor.

"I can't believe what happened to that poor girl. I was so shocked when Natasha told me about it," Franco said, shaking his head in dismay.

"Yes, it's absolutely terrible. She was so lovely." Anna started to tear up.

For a few moments, Franco was lost in thought. Finally, he spoke up. "Have they caught this maniac yet?" he asked as he handed Anna a handkerchief.

Overhearing everything, the usual commotion at the bookers' desk momentarily stopped and all eyes turned to Franco and Anna.

"No, and all of the models are so scared."

"What's taking the police so long?" Franco asked.

Anna was trying to compose herself, but Franco's last remark brought on a new flood of tears.

Shaking his head in sympathy, he put his hand on Anna's shoulder. "Don't cry, Anna, they'll catch him soon." He pulled her close for a sympathetic embrace, an embrace she was uncomfortable with. Her body stiffened from a knee-jerk reflex as she quickly stifled her tears and pulled away from him.

"Thank you, I appreciate that. So, um, where am I living?" she asked, changing the subject and drying her tears.

Silently enraged by her rebuff, Franco looked down and hid his expression. He didn't like being even mildly rejected. Managing to calm down, he looked back up and once again spoke in the charming voice the fashion world knew. "A wonderful residence called La Principessa. Many models live there, Anna. You will make many friends."

"Cool. By the way, is there a phone in the apartment?"

"A phone? Do you have someone special you need to call?" he asked.

"No, not really. Just my grandparents once in a while."

"Only your grandparents?"

"And my little brother." Anna's face lightened. Just speaking about her brother brought instant joy.

"Oh?" Franco was intrigued. "What about your parents?"

"My parents died when I was young."

"I see. So sorry to hear that," Franco said, unable to offer much empathy given his feelings for his own parents.

"What about a boyfriend?" he said coyly. "Doesn't a beautiful girl like you have someone special in her life?"

"No boyfriend yet." Embarrassed and uncomfortable once again, she continued. "I do want to phone my grandparents though, so how should I go about doing that?"

"Unfortunately, you'll have to go to the central post office because you can't make international phone calls from the apartment. This is Italy after all, not New York City."

"Oh. The post office?" Anna thought it was bizarre, but then again she really had no clue about how international communication worked.

"Yes, the post office. They have a section devoted to calling overseas," Franco said.

"OK, thanks. I'll figure it out."

Just then a beautiful, longhaired brunette model walked by and gave Franco a sexy smile. Franco blew her a kiss without missing a beat. "Later, darling," he said to the stunning young woman and then turned his attention back to Anna. "So, let's send you on your way, shall we."

He then looked over at Dawn, who was sitting at her desk going over charts. "Dawn, call a taxi for Anna." Franco then turned to Giacomo, who had been hovering close by. "Take Anna's luggage from the hall and put it in a taxi for her."

Giacomo, wasting no time, left to pick up Anna's suitcases and make his way down to wait for the taxi.

Turning back to Anna, Franco said, "There's a daytime doorman expecting you and he will give you your keys." He took her hand and led her out of the office into the hallway and pressed for the elevator.

"Thank you for everything, Franco. Should I come to the agency first thing tomorrow morning?"

"Actually, tonight I'm hosting a dinner at La Bella restaurant and I'd like you to be present. A lot of important photographers you should meet will be there."

"I see. You know, I'd love to, but I'm very tired."

"Anna, I only invite my favorites, and so far, you are one of them," Franco said, holding Anna's gaze. Although he was still smiling, his eyes had turned severe and his charming disposition dissipated.

"It's so nice of you to ask me, but can I make it another time? I'm exhausted," Anna said, unaware of his annoyance.

"You cannot," he said, the smile draining from his face. He stared intimidatingly into her eyes, secretly enjoying the discomfort emanating from one more beautiful girl's attempt to control her composure.

"Oh. I see," she said, surprised by this new, rather frightening side to Franco's character.

"We start late here, Anna. Plenty of time to rest."

"Of course," Anna said, compelled to agree.

"You must come. In fact, I will pick you up myself and take you there."

"OK then. What time?" she asked. Taken aback by Franco's character change, dark memories of her father's Dr. Jekyll/Mr. Hyde personality started to resurface.

"Nine p.m."

"Right. Nine p.m. then."

"Also, do wear something fabulous," Franco's said, once again oozing charm.

"Yes, of course." Anna walked into the elevator feeling depressed and angry with herself because she still couldn't stand up to this sort of guy. She had an amplified fear of intimidating men, especially men who had power over her. She wondered if it was caused by her father's drunken, rage-filled stupors, or was it simply because this man Franco had the ability to control her destiny, like it or not.

Lost in thought—anger with herself, to be more precise—she was startled when the elevator door opened on the ground floor.

"This way," Giacomo said, standing by ready to lead Anna to the waiting taxi.

"Oh, hello, Giacomo. Excuse me for jumping, but I forgot that you were going to help me with my luggage," Anna said in perfect Italian. She followed Giacomo as he led her to the waiting taxi and opened the door, allowing her to slip into the back seat.

"Thank you," she said.

As the taxi sped away, she leaned back against the seat, tired, in need of sleep and wishing desperately that Anika was sitting by her side ready to teach her how to deal with intimidating men—particularly ones who had all the power.

CHAPTER 16

BRUT GUY

"**S**o your sister went to Italy?" Detective Tansey asked, surprised that an eighteen-year-old girl would go to work in a foreign country just like that.

"My niece, not my sister," Mickey responded.

"Right, sorry. So when did she leave?"

"A week ago." Mickey wasn't necessarily pleased with the decision, but his parents seemed OK with it. To them, Milan, Italy, was a lot safer than New York City.

"Damn brave of her," Tansey said.

"I totally agree. But, like I said before, she speaks fluent Italian."

"I gotta tell ya, that's darned impressive."

"Yeah, well, my mom and pop emigrated from Sicily when they were in their twenties and they never did learn English very well, so we all speak Italian together."

"Interesting. I heard you went to Italy not too long ago, on a Mafia bust or something?"

"I'd ask how you found out, but I think I already know. Anyway, the Italian mob's alive and well, and when it stretches from the good ole USA over to the mother country, they call me in."

"I'll have to remember that."

Enough of this chitchat, Mickey thought, he wanted answers.

"So, what can I do for you, Gallo?"

"How're things goin' with the murder investigation? Got any suspects?"

"You mean, apart from you?"

"Knock it off," Mickey said. "Tell me what you got so far."

Tansey took a moment and gave Mickey the once-over, finally cracking a smile. "Guess I can do that, since you're one of us."

"Out with it," Mickey said. He and Tansey were on equal terms now, and Mickey wanted more information.

"We're workin' on a few leads."

"Such as?"

"Well, we called in that photographer you told us about. You know, Richie Rubin."

"How did that pan out?"

"Alibi's airtight."

"Really? Where was he?"

"Turns out he left Studio 54 with a gal named Lori. Later he was seen with her at the Mudd Club before gettin' on an early flight to Puerto Rico."

"Puerto Rico?"

"Yeah, he had a photography job down there, pictures for a new hotel in San Juan. Anyway, seems the guy never sleeps. A real cokehead."

"No surprise there. What about that guy Findler? You know, the one that harassed my niece at Bloomingdale's?"

"We looked into that too. Turns out he was shooting porn in Vegas. Smart girl, your niece. She knew he was a scumbag."

"Yeah, well, I drummed that into her head from the day she was born. And that guy—what's his name—you know, the guy with the restraining order?"

"Right, the burger flipper. Fatniski."

"Yeah, Fatniski. What about him? Did you find him?"

"Yup, we found him all right; in the hospital with both his legs slung up in casts. Turns out he got in a fight with the wrong person."

"Before or after the murder?"

"After."

"You think he mighta done it?"

"Doubt it. His alibi wasn't airtight, and his secretion count matched, but that's only an indicator. I have a hunch it's someone else."

"Why do you say that?"

"He's too stupid. I just think we're dealing with someone more sophisticated. Smarter, you know what I mean?"

"Yeah, I get it, but hunches can be wrong."

"True. Anyway, we'll catch the perp, just a matter of time."

"Hope it's before he kills again."

"Couldn't agree more."

"Whoever it is, you think this killer's the same guy who killed that girl, Rhonda?" Mickey asked, knowing that it was really too early to tell.

"You know how it is, Gallo. Could be a random coincidence, a copycat killer, pissed boyfriend—we're not sure yet."

"What about the taxi driver?"

"Clean as a whistle."

Mickey was discouraged, realizing the investigation was coming up short. "And the handbag?"

"Nothing."

"What about any other evidence?"

"C'mon, you know I'm not supposed to give you those kind of details," Tansey said.

The conversation hit a lull until Tansey remembered a piece of evidence he still needed to tackle. Against protocol, he decided to share it with Mickey. "Hey, maybe I do need help with something," Tansey said as he took out a list of the evidence found at the crime scene from his desk drawer and scrolled down it. "We found a hand-kerchief at the crime scene."

"I see. You think it's the perp's?"

"We do. It was right next to the victim's bed," Tansey said.

"Does it have markings or a label on it?"

"No, nothing. Just a plain white handkerchief."

"So, how can I help then?"

"Thing is, it has a very distinct smell. Sort of musky, but mixed with a spice or something."

"You think the smell could be from this guy's cologne?"

"I think so. It's not something I ever smelled before though. I don't know how to describe it other than to say it smells expensive. You know, sophisticated. That's why I have a hunch it's not this idiot Fatniski. He's clueless, not sophisticated at all. Just sick."

"I don't think I can help you with that if you say the smell is musky with a spice. Sounds unusual, and if it's the perp's cologne, as you think, I wouldn't have a clue. I'm a BRUT guy myself."

"Funny, me too," Tansey said. "Anyway, we've asked around and no one can place it."

"Well, if I think of anything, I'll let ya know."

Tansey scribbled his home number on a piece of paper and hand-ed it to Mickey. "Here's my home number. Call me anytime."

Mickey took the paper, put it in his pocket and stood up. He needed to get back to Port Chester. "Nice talkin' to ya."

CHAPTER 17

ANOTHER COUNTRY

A week had gone by since Anna arrived in Milan, and although everything was rather foreign to her, she managed quite well because she could speak the language. Despite the disconcerting arrival at Franco's Models, and the demanding social schedule that usually began right about when she preferred to tuck herself into bed with a good book, she was enjoying most of her new life. She loved her tiny little apartment, which was centrally located and near many quaint little food shops specializing in freshly made bread, pasta, perfectly ripened fruits and vegetables, delectable cheeses, and cured and aged meat of every type imaginable under the sun.

She took on with gusto her morning and late afternoon schedule of daily auditions spread throughout Milan, quickly learning the tram and bus system. The traditional lunch hour beginning at 1 p.m. and punctuated by siestas ending at 4 p.m.—a tradition her grandfather often longed for—gave her a wonderful opportunity to explore the ancient city, taking in the elaborate churches, historic landmarks, numerous cafes and cobblestone streets lined with Italianate buildings, many hiding private and sometimes elaborate interior courtyards.

Exploring the Italian culture, one so inherent to her upbringing, was a welcome diversion after Petra's murder.

Sunday had arrived, a day she had to herself, and despite the gloomy weather she ventured out and walked over to Piazza Del Duomo, featuring Milan's magnificent Cathedral. After spending more than an hour wandering around the centuries-old gothic structure, she wandered back through the throng of people in the enormous Italian square and headed down a side street leading toward the area of town she lived in.

A passing red Ferrari slowed down and pulled up alongside her. "Ciao, bella!"

Anna turned to see a stylish young blonde Italian man in designer sunglasses behind the wheel. She had no interest in starting up a conversation with the guy, even if he did have a Ferrari.

"Why is a beautiful lady like you alone on a Sunday afternoon?" he said in heavily accented English. A notorious playboy, experience convinced him she was a foreign fashion model. They all had a certain look.

Anna didn't know what to say. She was very uncomfortable and sensed he was leering at her with longing and desire in his eyes, something that seemed to happen to her a lot during her first week in Milan.

"I enjoy being alone," she said sharply in Italian. She continued to look straight ahead with the hopes that he would get the message and go away.

"You are very beautiful," he continued, completely taken aback by her use of Italian. He had never come across a model who spoke his language so well. All the models roaming the city were either American, Finnish or Swedish, and they all communicated in English. "Can I take you for a coffee?"

"No thanks," she said. *Oh no, he's not going away. Now what do I do?* If a shop were open she could duck inside one, but they were all closed. Anna continued looking straight ahead as she reached the crossing.

Suddenly a man called her name. She turned and saw a familiar face walking toward her. It was Paul. *What great timing. He must be back from the photo shoot in Sardinia that he told me about.*

"Hey, it's so nice to see you," he said, smiling ear to ear.

"You too, Paul. How was your location booking?"

"Fantastic! What a beautiful island. Basically, I had a vacation and got paid for it too. By the way, where are you living?" Paul asked.

"La Principessa. You?"

"Right around the corner at their sister residence."

"What? I didn't know they had one."

"Yeah, they do. Hey, can you believe we're actually working here in Milan?" Paul said as the two walked together.

"I know, it's amazing." Anna noticed from the corner of her eye that the defeated man in the Ferrari had finally pulled away. "Finally," she said, relieved.

"Huh?"

"That car, the red one. It's finally gone."

"I noticed that guy and his flashy car. Was he a friend of yours?"

"No. I have no idea who he was. He wouldn't leave me alone."

"Guess he liked you."

"Well, I didn't like him. Anyway, your timing was perfect."

Paul and Anna continued walking on, suddenly having so much in common because of the move to Italy. Unaware that a black cloud was hovering above, they chitchatted about their future plans until a crack of lightning filled the sky.

"Oh, no! I think it's going to pour." As soon as Anna said it, the skies opened up and a torrent of rain came down. "Darn, I don't have an umbrella," Anna said.

"Me either. Let's run. I live right over there."

The two of them ran toward Paul's residence and stood under the overhang. It was coming down hard, so Paul suggested they go up to his apartment instead of standing in the lobby and waiting it out. Anna liked Paul. He was nice, friendly and easygoing. She also liked the way he looked. She found his mysterious blue eyes, moustache and beard, and athletic body very attractive.

"This way," Paul said, unlocking the entry door. He held the heavy glass and metal door open and allowed Anna to enter the building first.

"You don't have a reception desk?" Anna asked.

"No. This is a residence for men, so I guess they feel we don't need one." Paul led the way through the dimly lit lobby of dull, painted concrete up a few dirty marble stairs and down an even darker hall.

"It's so dark and dank. Ours is much nicer, sorry to say."

"Well, you know how it is in the modeling world. You women get a much better deal. You're even paid more per hour."

"Do we? I didn't know that," Anna said innocently.

"Yeah, but it's OK. I'm just happy to have the opportunity to travel the world."

"Well, it's probably the only industry where such a thing happens."

"True. Follow me, I'm at the back of this long hall."

"Hope your apartment is nicer than the hallway," Anna said jokingly.

"Not much, but at least we can dry off. Also, I have American coffee. Would you like a cup?"

"Sure." Anna didn't have the heart to tell him that she really preferred espresso. Anyway, she could use the hot liquid to warm up.

Paul opened the door and switched on the light.

Anna breathed in a strong smell. "Smells good in here," she said. "Much better than the hallway."

"You like it?"

"Yeah, I recognize it. I know I've smelled it before. What is it? A candle or something?"

"No, my new cologne. I thought I'd try to be a bit more sophisticated when I go on auditions now that I'm heading for the big time." Paul winked, joking of course.

They took off their coats and shook off the rain before Paul hung them up in the foyer closet.

"Have a seat. I'll be back in a jiffy," he said, pointing to a beige and brown sofa.

"Sure. Thanks." Anna suddenly realized that she had followed a guy she hardly knew into his apartment in a very dark building in a foreign country. Was she nuts? A chill went up her spine. He's from New York City after all. Could he be the murderer? No way, he's too nice.

"Here you go," Paul said moments later as he came out of the kitchen and handed Anna a large cup of steaming-hot liquid.

"Thanks." Anna took the coffee, thinking it could be the perfect weapon if need be.

"So, do you miss New York?" she asked, sipping from the cup.

"I do a bit, but I'm kinda glad to have gotten away."

"Really, why is that?"

Paul sank in his chair. "Well, the truth is, it wouldn't have been long before the cops called me in about Petra's murder."

Anna choked on her coffee and her face drained of all color as the pit of her stomach cinched together into a nauseous knot.

CHAPTER 18

VANILLA

Mickey drove cautiously along the snowy street toward his modest home in the heart of Port Chester. He pulled into his driveway, fumbling the keys as he got out of the car. It was late, and he was exhausted after meeting Tansey in New York City and then working on a case in Port Chester until the early morning hours. Relieved that he now had an entire week off, all he wanted to do was unwind, have a beer and hit the sack. He unlocked the door and went inside. After taking off his coat, he made his way into the kitchen, grabbed a beer out of the fridge and popped open a can of his favorite drink. He took a long, lingering gulp of the creamy liquid. He stood there enjoying his beer and momentarily letting go of the cruel world he had to deal with on a daily basis, but it wasn't long before he started racking his brain about Petra's murder, and Ben Fatniski. Tansey didn't think the guy was her killer, but Mickey wasn't so sure. It was true Fatniski was a greasy dimwit, but Mickey wanted to know more. He decided he was going to go talk to Fatniski himself. He took the last swig of beer, crushed the can and threw it in the trash, then went up to bed.

Several hours passed before a stream of light shined through the airy white curtains and rested on his buff, olive-skinned torso peeking out from under a white duvet. He tossed and turned, slowly opening his eyes around 11:30 a.m. It was Sunday and he didn't need to get up, so he crossed his arms behind his head and continued dozing. Ten minutes turned into thirty, thirty into forty, and then suddenly Mickey's eyes opened wide and he bolted upright.

"Franco!" he shouted.

He checked his clock radio—February18th, 12:30 p.m.—then jumped out of bed, naked apart from his tighty-whities, and ran to his kitchen desk. Scrambling for his phonebook in the useless papers stacked high, he berated himself for not being more organized. He finally pulled it out of the heap and frantically began flipping pages until he found Natasha's number and dialed her Greenwich home. No answer. "C'mon, c'mon," he said, clicking the receiver button several times until he heard a new dial tone. Becoming more agitated and impatient by the second, he furiously dialed her townhouse.

"Hello?"

"Natasha, this is Mickey, Anna McKenna's uncle."

A few moments of silence passed. "Surprised to hear your voice," she said.

"Was Franco Rubelli in New York City when that model Rhonda was murdered last April?" Mickey asked, urgently getting to the point.

"What?" Natasha was completely taken aback by the question.

"Natasha, tell me!" Mickey said, raising his voice.

"OK, OK. Let me think a minute."

Moments passed, causing Mickey to really lose his cool. "Natasha, hurry up!"

"Yes, I remember now. He was in New York City scouting models. Why?"

"When I met him at Studio 54 the night of your party, I vaguely remember smelling something odd, something like vanilla."

"He always smells of Vanilla Musk. I think it's his signature cologne."

"I thought so."

"I'm not following you, Mickey. Why is this so important?"

"It just is," he said, not wanting to divulge information about evidence from the investigation.

"What are you getting at?"

"Natasha, I think he killed Rhonda and Petra."

"Oh my gosh! And Anna's there," Natasha said, the blood draining from her face.

"Let me go, I'm gonna call the agency right away," Mickey said.

"But no one's there. It's Sunday."

"Oh shit! OK, gotta go." Mickey slammed down the phone and went to the hall closet, fumbling through his coat pockets until he found the piece of paper with Detective Tansey's home number scribbled on it. He ran back to the kitchen and dialed Tansey.

"Frank Tansey."

"Tansey, this is Mickey Gallo. It's vanilla."

"Huh? What the hell you talkin' about?"

"The smell on the handkerchief, it's Vanilla Musk and Franco Rubelli, that Italian agent, is the killer."

"Hang on, hang on. How do you know that?"

"It just came to me this morning. I remember now that when I met this guy at Studio 54 I smelled something distinct, something strange. Spicy and musky, just like you described."

"Yeah?"

"It's his signature cologne. Natasha from Top Form Management just told me."

"The owner, right?"

"Right, and she confirmed that Franco was scouting models in New York City when that girl Rhonda was murdered. He's the guy. I feel it in my gut."

"Holy crap! Isn't your niece over in Milan?"

"Yes, she is. We don't have a minute to lose."

"Right. OK," was all Tansey could say. Italy, he thought. What the hell did he know about Italy.

"I'm calling the cops in Milan. I'll call you back."

"Wait a minute," Tansey said. "This is my investigation, I'm making the phone call."

"Yeah, but you don't speak Italian and most Italian cops don't speak English." Mickey was annoyed. Tansey was acting like a typical detective, possessive of his turf.

After a long pause, Tansey spoke up. "Right. You have a point there. You call, but call me back as soon as possible."

Mickey slammed down the phone and dialed the international operator.

"Operator, how can I help you?" a cheery female voice said.

"This is Detective Mickey Gallo and I need the phone number of police headquarters in Milan."

"One moment please."

Mickey drummed his fingers impatiently on the kitchen table. The cops needed to arrest this son of a bitch as soon as possible, Mickey thought. C'mon, hurry it up.

"I have two numbers for you, detective. Do you have a pen?"

"Yeah. Shoot." He scribbled down the numbers.

"Shall I connect you?"

"Right away."

"Hold a moment please."

"I'm sorry, that line is busy," the operator said.

"OK, dial the next one."

The same thing happened.

"I'm still getting a busy signal detective. You can continue dialing yourself if you have international capabilities."

Shit, Mickey thought. *Of course I don't.*

"No, operator, please continue trying. This is an emergency."

Fifteen minutes passed and the operator still couldn't get through. "Excuse me, officer, but there must be some problem. I can get through to Italy, but it's the actual police station that keeps giving me the busy signal."

"Dammit! Why the fuck are they tying up the phone lines!"

"Excuse me?" The operator was appalled by Mickey's language, but she had heard everything throughout her career.

"Look, forget it. Just forget it." Mickey slammed down the phone and called Tansey back.

"I can't get through. The operator tried for more than twenty minutes and she kept getting a busy signal."

"Shit," Tansey said.

"Shit is right. Something must be up over there," Mickey said, unaware that most of the Milanese police force had been called away from the station because of an emergency on a main street in Milan, leaving the few left at the station overwhelmed with calls about the situation. "Look, we have no time to lose. I'm going to get on a plane and go over there."

"Hey, I trust you and your gut. I'll speak to my sergeant and yours and see if they can pull a few strings with the lieutenants and get you reimbursed for the flight and hotel. If you're up to it, go."

"As you said, my niece is over there. I'm gonna head out the door soon so you keep trying the police over in Italy." Mickey gave Tansey the two numbers and hung up. He quickly showered and was out the door heading for JFK in no time, figuring he'd find a flight once he got there. One of the airlines had to be leaving on Sunday afternoon.

Traffic was heavy for some reason, which didn't help Mickey's nerves, but eventually he made it to the airport and over to the woman behind the information desk.

"Is Alitalia the only airline left with a flight to Italy this afternoon?" Mickey asked the agent.

"Yes, sir. Flights on other airlines have already departed, but Alitalia is due to depart in forty minutes. You're just in time if you'd like to take it."

"Yes, put me on. Any seat."

"You'll have to go to the Alitalia ticket counter over in section B."

"You can't issue a ticket for me?"

"No, sorry. As I said, you'll have to go over to Alitalia."

Mickey picked up his carry-on bag and ran toward section B. He pulled out his badge, thinking it could come in handy, and cut in front of the line. "I need to get on the next flight to Milan."

No one in line dared say anything, their eyes now glued to Mickey and what was going on.

"You're just in time, officer," the agent said as she glanced at the badge.

"I know, I know. Just get me on the flight please."

He pulled out a lump of cash—he always kept five grand stashed in an empty can of peanuts—and handed the ticketing agent the money for the fare. She issued him a ticket and told him he needed to go see the agent at the check-in counter. Does this ever end, Mickey thought as he headed over. Sweating profusely and moving quickly, he held out his badge, lending credence to his lack of composure, and once again went to the front of the line. Everyone in the area knew something was going on and swiftly got out of his way. Mickey checked in, rushed through security and arrived at the gate fifteen minutes before departure. Everyone had already boarded, but Mickey, spotting a telephone booth nearby, decided to call Tansey first to see if he got through to the police department in Milan.

"Frank Tansey."

"Hey, it's Gallo. Did you get through?"

"I did, but the sons of bitches rattled off in Italian. I couldn't understand a word they said."

"Dammit. What did I tell ya."

A woman's voice came over the loudspeaker, making it impossible to hear Tansey.

"Hang on," Mickey said.

"Alitalia flight 464 is ready for departure for Milan. Please make your way to gate sixteen immediately." The woman repeated the final boarding call in Italian.

During the announcement, Mickey thought about whether he should call his mother and father, fill them in on what was happening and have them call the police in Milan. Because they speak Italian, are Italian, they could explain everything and ask the cops to check into Anna's whereabouts. Doubtful they'd check out Rubelli though.

Suddenly, Mickey realized the woman on the loudspeaker was specifically requesting that Mickey Gallo immediately report to the gate. Between the fact that there was no time and he'd freak out his parents, he decided not to call them. The announcement finally ended and Mickey wrapped up his conversation with Tansey.

"Gotta go, the flight's takin' off. I'll be in touch." Mickey hung up and ran to the gate just as they were closing the doors. Because he hadn't checked in any bags, they were prepared to take off without him.

"Mickey Gallo?" a striking redheaded female flight attendant asked.

"That's right." Mickey was still holding his badge as they led him through the door down the corridor and sat him in first class. Nice surprise, he thought, and sat back in his seat. Exhausted, he closed his eyes and before long was fast asleep.

CHAPTER 19

A CRUSH

Monday morning arrived soon enough, but not before Anna and Paul got to know each other better. Although she'd been prepared to use her steaming hot coffee to hit Paul in the face if he attempted to hurt her, she never needed to. Once Paul sensed her terror when he mentioned that the NYPD would most likely call him in to interrogate him sooner or later about Petra's murder, he explained why. He told her he had met Rhonda right before she was murdered and the NYPD called him in after that, thinking he could have been involved. He did his best to reassure her of his complete innocence and told her what he told the police—he was in Queens with his friend, Danny, and the two of them were helping his mother with work around her house.

They talked a lot about the gruesome murders of both Petra and Rhonda, and Anna spent a good deal of time crying. Paul consoled her, and although she remained on guard the whole time she sat out the rain, she convinced herself that he couldn't possibly be the killer. Besides, the night of Top Form's party at Studio 54 she remembered seeing him and meeting his friend Danny. She believed Paul when he said that Danny came to meet him there because they were heading over to Hunter Mountain that night to go skiing for the rest of the weekend. Based on that, and her strong intuition, she decided to trust him. So much so, they even shared a kiss before he gallantly walked her back to her residence after the storm.

He's such a lovely guy, Anna thought as she got ready for her big day. In a few hours, she would be modeling for Federico in the first show of Milan Fashion Week, which was taking place at a spectacular venue. Although she had practiced the mechanisms of twisting and turning for a runway show, taught to her by one of the bookers at Top Form, and although she had already done a fashion show in New York and turned out to be a natural despite her clumsiness, she was extremely nervous just the same. Not only was it her first booking in Milan, it happened to be for the hottest designer in Italy, in the world for that matter.

Paul, who was in the show as its token male model, offered to meet up with Anna at her apartment and take the subway together to the event. He announced himself to the porter, who gave him an indifferent once-over, and took the elevator to Anna's floor and rang the doorbell.

Paul smiled approvingly when Anna opened the door. "Good morning."

"Almost ready. Let me grab my bag and we can be on our way," she said.

The two, now officially enamored with each other, talked enthusiastically the entire time it took to descend into the subway, hop on the train, and reach their destination.

"Another day, another dollar, or lira to be precise," Paul said.

The two grabbed their belongings, exited the train and walked up the stairs to a busy tree-lined piazza featuring the beautiful white neoclassical building where the show was being held. They met up with a few other models on their way to the same place, and together the group, many in sunglasses to hide their bare, makeup-free faces and to add cache to the mystery surrounding their extraordinary lives, walked up the stairs, through a reception area, and directly into a huge 3000-square-foot room.

Anna stared at the recessed ceiling, large chandeliers, and long, pristine, white runway flanked by gold-gilded guest chairs, empty apart from the few half-asleep models waiting for instructions. Loud instrumental disco music filled the air as the crew adjusting the sound system worked in tandem with the rest of the production team. Anna and Paul, along with the incoming group of girls, made their way to the seats, plopped their bags down and joined the others waiting for instructions. It was going to be a long morning of rehearsals and hair and makeup, culminating with the fashion show at 11:30 a.m. After a short wait, the producer called all the models backstage to begin rehearsal, which turned out to be incredibly intense due to problems with the lighting and music, and the hottest Italian fashion designer's ego.

After two hours of rehearsal, time Paul spent mostly reading apart from the occasional instances when he was required to escort a model down the runway, all of the models were instructed to go backstage for hair and makeup. Transformed by 11:00 a.m., a gaggle of made-up and coiffed models emerged and stood at the top of the runway chitchatting until it was time to change. Some puffed on cigarettes in an effort to calm nerves, stifle appetites or just be amazingly cool.

"Here comes Franco," one of the models said.

All the models turned to see the prancing peacock enter the enormous room and preen his way over to the gorgeous group, where he affectionately kissed each model on both cheeks. Saying hello in Italy to familiar faces, friends and family was an ordeal, and one that

Americans found a bit daunting since no one in the US greeted each other with air kisses.

"Don't be nervous, girls. But if you are, just fake it. You hear me? Fake it until you make it," Franco said, instructing his girls on how to remain calm and cool.

"Fake it 'til you make it. Fake it 'til you make it." A chant started as a few giggling models chimed in. The excitement was palpable, even if some of the models weren't new to the world of high fashion runway shows.

"Franco, my legs are shaking," one of the newer models said as she took a long drag on her cigarette.

Franco turned toward Dawn, who had showed up alongside him. "Get the girls some champagne," he said.

Dawn didn't react right away. Even though the models needed to relax, she was unsure about giving them champagne so early in the morning. Many hadn't eaten a thing yet. Certainly the champagne would go to their heads, possibly causing them to be off balance on the runway.

"What are you waiting for?" Franco was irritated. He expected Dawn to follow his orders immediately, and without question.

"Right away," Dawn said, despite her concerns. She didn't want to make Franco angry, and the truth was she couldn't care less about whether the models got drunk. What she did care about was protecting Franco from making a mistake. Little did he know, she watched his every move like a hawk. She was obsessed with him and hoped one day he would realize how much she cared about him. How much he needed her.

"One glass is all you get for now," Franco said. "Tonight I'm taking you girls to dinner at La Bella. Then we're going to Nepentha, where you can dance and drink to your hearts' content."

"Huh?" Anna said, glancing at Paul, who was now standing among the group.

Franco turned specifically to her and glared into her eyes. "Yes, Federico is throwing a party and everyone must come. This is business. I don't care whether you have a booking early tomorrow morning or not."

Anna was speechless. She was beginning to despise this man who wielded all of the power over her career. She hated playing his sick game, but knew she had to for her family. For Joey.

Dawn returned with a tray of filled champagne flutes. "Champagne for everybody," she said.

"OK, girls, take a glass, drink up and then get backstage and change into your first outfit. The guests are arriving soon," Franco said, ignoring the fact that Paul was a male model.

"Yes, boss," the models said, laughing together.

Franco considered one small glass of the delicious bubbly to be the best medicine to calm and loosen nerves and help the models glide serenely down the runway without staring out like deer in headlights at the bright lights glaring into their eyes and clumsily running into each other.

Snuffing out cigarettes, sipping the last of their champagne and putting their glasses on the tray, the girls began walking backstage, now invigorated and ready to perform.

"And don't forget," Franco commanded. "You are Franco's models, the most beautiful girls on the planet!"

CHAPTER 20

THE LONG FLIGHT

Mickey sat straight up, ready to jump off the plane the minute it touched down. He was a bag of nerves, compounded one hundred fold by the delayed takeoff, constant turbulence and stormy weather they had endured over the Atlantic. The plane, which was supposed to have landed at 8:00 a.m. but by now was more than an hour late, started circling over the city of Milan.

Why aren't we landing? What the hell is going on? I need to get off this plane and track down Anna. Mickey was not only agitated, he was furious.

Exasperated, he looked out the window and peered through the heavy rain and dismal fog hovering over the city, then looked at his watch and changed it to Italian time. Irritated, he reached up and pressed the overhead button for the flight attendant, who quickly, and happily, came to his side.

Without giving her a chance to speak, he blurted out in perfect Italian to the hovering redhead, "What's going on, we're late."

"I'm sorry, Mr. Gallo, we're circling. We can't land yet."

"I know we're circling. Why?"

"We have to stay above the storm until it passes," the attractive flight attendant said uneasily.

"What? It's just rain, isn't it?" Mickey looked out the window again. This time he noticed the huge dark cloud below crackling with lightning. "Oh. OK. Got it." Resigned to the situation, he gave up and leaned back in his seat.

Twenty minutes later the captain came over the intercom and asked all flight attendants to prepare for landing. The storm had finally passed by. The plane landed without incident, but then it just sat on the tarmac. Once again Mickey pressed the call button and the attentive redhead came to his side. He looked at her impatiently without saying a word.

"I'm sorry, sir, but most of the ground service we have here at the airport are on strike, so we have to wait before we can get to a gate and disembark," she said, clearly embarrassed about this new complication.

"On strike?"

"Yes, two of the three ground service unions went on strike last night. I wasn't aware of it until now," the flight attendant said, annoyed by her country's actions. "This is Italy. We have a lot of strikes by unhappy workers these days."

"Shit!" Mickey said in English, startling the flight attendant. She was used to swear words in Italian but didn't hear them often in English. Nevertheless, she understood fully his frustration. Her entire country was frustrated, and in turmoil. It seemed that everyone was unhappy.

"Right, and so how long will we sit here, may I ask?"

"I don't know," she said, scrunching up her face apologetically.

"Of course," Mickey said sarcastically. Dismayed and disgusted, he couldn't help thinking to himself how much he loved the food, wine and enormous generosity of spirit in his motherland, but didn't question for a minute why his parents left. Endearing to some, chaos was the best way to describe one of the most beautiful and culturally rich countries in the world.

"Once again, I apologize for the delay. Can I help you with anything else?" the flight attendant inquired sympathetically.

"Look, I'm a detective with the New York Police Department and I'm working on a very serious case. I need to get off this plane as soon as possible," Mickey said, pulling out his badge in the hopes of speeding up the situation.

"I understand, sir, but we're in the middle of the tarmac and we don't have any jet stairs in place so you can get off," the flight attendant said sympathetically. She wasn't sure if she believed this supposed detective, but was completely intrigued—he was extremely handsome, powerful and probably unmarried because he didn't have a ring on his finger.

Mickey was enraged and terrified that he wasn't going to find this sleazebag modeling agent before the day was over, which meant another night would pass before the guy was behind bars. "Let me talk to the captain. This is urgent."

"One moment please, let me see if I can get him for you," she said.

She wiggled her way seductively through the aisle, but Mickey didn't even notice. He just wanted to get off the damn plane. After a few moments, the chief flight attendant, referred to as the purser, came back and told Mickey that there wasn't much that could be done and that he needed to be patient. Mickey showed the purser his badge and then, without naming names, explained to him in detail about the murders of two young women in New York City and why he had come to Italy.

"Didn't you speak with the police force in Milan before you got on this plane?" the purser asked.

"I called yesterday. Several times."

"And?"

"It was constantly busy!"

Fortunately, the purser believed him. Although it would have been unusual for the phone lines to the police department to be continually busy, he knew that anything could happen in Italy these days. "Give me a minute," he said and walked to the cockpit to have a word with the captain. The captain listened to the sinister story and decided to radio the control tower about the urgency of Mickey's situation. Several minutes passed before the chief controller made the situation a priority. The purser walked back to where Mickey sat nervously tapping his foot with his arms crossed and an annoyed expression on his face.

"Mr. Gallo, the captain has spoken to the control tower and they're taking your situation seriously and alerting the police."

Mickey sighed with relief. "Thanks. I really appreciate it. By the way, do you have a phone in the cockpit that I can use?"

"No, but if you really need to speak to someone we can put you through to the control tower, who can then call on your behalf and connect you."

Mickey thought about this for a moment. Who was he going to call? He didn't have Anna's phone number, just her address, and although he did have her agency's phone number, what was he going to say? Your boss is a killer? Who would believe him? And what about his Italian? It was very good, but he was still a foreigner in a foreign country. Would this whole situation get lost in translation?

The purser waited patiently for an answer until Mickey, knowing that the evidence showed that the killer—Franco Rubelli, to be more precise—seemed to kill at night and that it was only 10:30 a.m., decided not to involve the control tower any more than he already had. He didn't want to create panic and more chaos than already existed, sure that it would just make matters worse than they already were.

"Thanks, never mind," Mickey said.

"I understand. Let me know if you need anything else." The purser headed back up the aisle and into the cockpit.

Totally exasperated, Mickey sat back in his seat and let out a long sigh. *When is this going to end?* He closed his eyes and rested his head against the seat. *And when am I going to get to Anna's apartment? I need to get to her as soon as possible, before I do anything else.* He bent down and grabbed his duffle bag, which was squashed under the seat in front of him, and began rummaging through it until he finally found a note with Anna's new Italian address scribbled on it. He put her address in his pocket and continued thinking about the plan he had come up with earlier. If she wasn't there, he'd get the police to take him to Franco Rubelli's agency. Mickey knew he needed to convince the police to bring this guy Rubelli in and lock him up, before he murdered again.

CHAPTER 21

A FASHION SHOW

The deafening disco music slowly came to an end while the bright lights faded and the last willowy model of the scene stopped, gently pivoted and gracefully exited off the runway to her left behind a wall. Then, like lightning, she swiftly vaulted down the set of steps to the exhilarating chaos backstage. Twelve models, twelve dressers, the designer and his team of stylists, the makeup and hair team, and members of the production team were all frantically going about their business amongst the fifty outfit ensembles lined up on six clothing racks, all of which were stuffed into a 30x12 foot space behind the large white stage backdrop. Clothes were flying everywhere as panicked dressers scrambled to help models tear off their outfits and put on the next one.

Anna was frantically rushing to zip up her last outfit, a stunningly beautiful emerald-green velvet gown, while her dresser sat on the floor and buckled up her coordinating delicate gold sandals. Once on, Anna lifted her gown and, trying desperately not to trip, briskly maneuvered through the posse of people backstage toward the lineup and found her place in first position near the four steps leading up to the stage entrance. Knowing that she and Paul were due to open the gown scene had her stomach queasy from nerves. She tried to relax her breathing down to a snail's pace while a hairdresser coiffed her hair, a makeup artist powdered her face and a stylist scrambled for earrings in response to the nervous designer's screeching orders. Suddenly, Paul, dashing in a striking, high-fashion tuxedo, was by her side.

"Hey, beautiful."

"Hey there," she replied bashfully.

"You guys are next," a woman from the production team said.

Paul and Anna carefully and quietly climbed the four steps and stood right behind the director's assistant behind the wall camouflaging the stage entrance. The director's assistant was taking cues via headphones from the director stationed up in a small inconspicuous open space on the mezzanine level at the far end of the enormous room. Anna could see the last model on the runway strike a pose as the music and lights faded out behind her and she swiftly left the stage. The director's assistant received a cue and then looked back over to Paul and Anna and gave them the OK to begin.

Terrified, Anna gingerly grabbed ahold of her gown and followed Paul out onto the pitch-black stage and struck the elegant pose they had practiced during rehearsal. Still as a statue, flowing fog generated from a dry ice machine gently rose around them in sync with the emergence of soft, slowly intensifying music and a gradually increasing spotlight. The effect was surreal and the audience loved it. Suddenly the music heightened and the introduction of loud percussions prompted Anna and Paul to begin gliding down the runway. The audience erupted into cheers. The newest Italian designer on the block was a superstar, and Anna had just helped elevate him to new heights. Paul escorted her down the runway twice, stopping and allowing Anna to twirl and pose for the posse of photographers snapping away. A natural, Anna did a great job of hiding her nerves. Soon they headed back to the top of the runway, where the next model stood stationary, striking a dramatic pose and ready to spring to life and strut the runway with Paul once Anna walked offstage behind the exit wall.

"Stay in your last outfit," a woman from the production team said as Anna made her way down the stairs to the backstage chaos.

Yippee! The show is almost over, Anna thought. *Modeling in a fashion show isn't too hard after all. It's fun actually, a real adrenaline rush!*

The next model came off stage and lined up behind Anna, followed by the next one and the next one. Before long, most of the models stood waiting for the remaining ones to finish onstage and get in line in preparation for the finale. It was the first moment they had to actually breath normally during the whole show. Excited, in line, and waiting for the finale to begin so all the models could strut the runway one last time, the ending buzz left the models cheerful and full of energy.

"I want more champagne," one of the Dutch models said, totally energized by the show and ready to do another one.

"Me too. I'm loving champagne," the only Italian model said in strongly accented English.

"I can't wait to go dancing tonight," piped in an American model.

"Me either," a model from Sweden chimed in.

Anna turned to the American model behind her, a striking young woman with ebony skin and piercing catlike green eyes. "Are you going?"

"Of course I'm going. Besides, there's no choice. Franco calls all of the shots."

"I don't really want to go," Anna said, to no one in particular.

"Do you want to work?" the American model said, aghast.

The lights and the soft music began to fade, signaling the end of the show, as Paul and a stunning Swedish model adorned in an outlandishly embellished wedding dress reached the top of the runway and struck a pose. The lights swiftly went back on full force and Donna Summer's latest disco hit began blaring full throttle out of the loud speakers as the finale began.

"Hey, girls, let's boogey," one of the girls said.

Instantly several of the models began gyrating and clapping to the music as the assistant director ushered then onstage so they could strut the runway one more time for the finale before taking their designated position in order to welcome the designer on stage. The audience was on their feet clapping wildly for the hottest designer in Milan, who eventually appeared on the stage and bashfully walked down the runway to resounding applause. Before long, the entire posse of models gathered around him and clapped enthusiastically along with the audience to show their profound respect.

The show was over, but the buzz and energy was just beginning for the girls.

CHAPTER 22

PROTOCOL

Mickey checked his watch. It was 11:30 a.m. and he was still on the plane. Shaking his head in frustration, he put his elbow on the armrest and placed his chin in the palm of his hand, letting out a long sigh while he stared out the window onto the gloomy tarmac. Everything was at a standstill. Planes filled with passengers weren't moving and abandoned jet stairs, clearly left by transportation personnel, sat haphazardly around the expansive tarmac. Unsure of his next move, Mickey closed his eyes and momentarily drifted off. He was mentally exhausted, not just from this unforeseen complication, but also from the frightening flight.

A few moments later he felt someone tapping on his shoulder. He opened his eyes to find the redheaded flight attendant bending over him.

"Detective, quietly get your bag and come with me to the back of the plane," she whispered in a barely audible voice.

Mickey understood and stood up. He discreetly put on his green leather jacket, put his duffle bag over his shoulder and followed the flight attendant while she maneuvered unobtrusively through the aisles of the new jumbo jet past annoyed, exhausted passengers and the last curtained galley and toward the final exit door on the left, which was used primarily to receive catering deliveries and supplies.

"The captain managed to get emergency ground support for this situation," the flight attendant said as they reached the purser, who was standing by the opened exit door.

"Detective Gallo, the police are waiting for you." The purser motioned toward the exit door and the portable aircraft steps that had been put in place for the unique situation.

"Thank you very much. I really appreciate your extra effort in this situation," Mickey said as he disembarked the plane and headed down the stairs to the waiting police car, a small green Alfa Romeo with the word *Polizia* written in white letters across the door. Mickey broke into the first smile he'd had in more than forty-eight hours.

Three policemen, two of whom were obvious police officers dressed in slick-belted black leather jackets, grey trousers and black police berets with striking gold emblems in the center, and the airport police commissary, wearing a well-cut, dark-gray Italian suit and coordinating tie under a beige, belted trench coat, were standing next to the police car.

"Hi, I'm Detective Gallo," Mickey said in Italian once he reached the ground. He reached out and shook the hand of the officer dressed in civilian clothes.

"Good morning. Officer Ferrari, airport police commissary."

"Nice to meet you," Mickey said.

"And this is Officer Bianchi and Officer Romano," Ferrari continued.

"Can't tell you how great it is to see you all. Thanks a lot for getting me off that damn plane."

"Always happy to help a fellow Italian," Ferrari said.

Despite their defeat by the allies in World War II and the communist sentiments brought on by the extreme left wing organization called the Red Brigades, most Italians admired everything about America. And if one happened to be American-Italian, all the better. They were welcomed into the country like long-lost family who immigrated to the US in the late 1800s.

Certain that the guys were eager to hear the full story, Mickey began giving a brief synopsis about the two gruesome murders in New York City and how the actual killer was living in Milan. "Listen, I want to explain everything to you, but I really need to get to the center of Milan. Every minute counts," Mickey said.

"Understood, but we first need to stop at the police office in the airport," Ferrari said.

Mickey hadn't considered this on the plane. Of course, he thought, why should they believe him outright? If some guy landed in the US claiming to be a detective, the airport police would first have to investigate and make sure the guy was telling the truth and wasn't some lunatic fabricating a story.

"We'll need to get in touch with the Police Commissioner's office in Milan. Chances are they'll need to speak with the US Consulate and verify everything before we get an OK to proceed," Ferrari said.

"Yes, of course, we'd do the same," Mickey said, his enthusiasm now deflated as he realized it was going to take some time before he could get the police on board and help him catch Rubelli.

"Glad you understand. Hop in." Ferrari opened the door of the squad car. Tiny in comparison to American squad cars, Mickey had no choice but to squeeze into the backseat. They sped away, maneuvering through the randomly parked planes and airport chaos toward the airport police station. A few minutes later the officers got out of the car and led Mickey to the dingy office, subtly making sure to surround him in the event he might want to make a run for it.

"Have a seat," Ferrari said after the team reached a quiet office much like the ones back home. "So, Detective Gallo, give me all of your details so we can get the ball rolling."

"Sure, no problem. The sooner the better." Mickey wrote down all the pertinent information the Italian police force would need to give to the United States Consulate to confirm his identity, and then suggested they start with Detective Tansey. "Detective Tansey is the detective heading up the investigation into the two murders in New York City. He'll be the best one to speak with regarding the case."

"OK. Why don't you sit tight while we work on this." Ferrari turned to Officer Bianchi and asked him to get some sandwiches and coffee. "This is going to take a bit of time. Can we get you a sandwich or something?" Ferrari asked Mickey.

"Sure, why not. Anything's fine," Mickey said as he looked down at his watch. It was already close to 1 p.m. Exasperated, he nonetheless kept his cool. Nothing could be done to rush the process. This is how it was, and this is how it had to be.

⋏

"Detective Gallo?" Ferrari said as he walked into the office a few hours later. "We have good news. Everything checked out, as I knew it would, and we have a detective team heading this way to pick you up. They'll be here in a few minutes."

"Fantastic. In the meantime, can we track down the number to this apartment building called La Principessa?" Mickey said as he stood up. "It's the residence my niece is living in and I want to call over there to see if she's there."

"No problem," Ferrari said. "Give me a minute." He walked out of the office and less than a minute later came back in with the phone number to La Principessa's porter. He picked up the receiver on the black rotary dial telephone and dialed the number. The line was busy. He hung up and dialed again. Still busy. He called the operator, explained the situation and the operator investigated. A minute later she back on the line.

"I'm sorry officer, the phone line is down and not scheduled for repair for a few days," the operator said.

"Of course," Ferrari said sarcastically. He hung up the phone and turned to Mickey.

"Typical. The line is down."

"Damn it!" Mickey's hope of finding Anna right away had just been quashed, adding to his nerves.

"Sorry about that." Ferrari crossed his arms, looked down and shook his head in disgust. Then a thought came into his mind. "By the way, I want to ask you something. Why didn't you phone Police Headquarters in Milan before you got on the plane? It would have saved you a lot of time. They would have met you at the plane and taken you straight to Milan."

"I did, for fifteen damn minutes, but the operator kept getting a busy signal."

"Impossible. It's Police Headquarters. You can always get through."

"Well, I'm telling you, the US operator couldn't," Mickey said, irritated all over again just thinking about it.

"When did you call?" Ferrari asked.

"Yesterday. Sunday."

"Hmmm. What time?"

"Let me think a minute." Mickey made the calculation in his mind and added the six hours to New York time. "It would have been early evening, about 7- 7:15 p.m. in Milan."

Officer Ferrari thought back to last night and then it became clear. There was no doubt in his mind that the telephone lines were tied up because of the chaos taking place on one of the swankiest streets in Milan at the time Gallo tried to call.

"Oh, man. We have to apologize, but last night at that time a crime scene was taking place on one of Milan's main streets."

Mickey's curiosity was peaked as he looked at Ferrari eagerly for more information.

"When you called, a well-known Italian industrialist had just been kidnapped and four of his bodyguards killed by the Red Brigades. I suspect the entire police staff was working on that," Ferrari said.

"Are you kiddin' me?"

"No, I wish I was. You've heard about the Red Brigades, right?"

"Sure, sure. They're that paramilitary group responsible for a lot of murders and kidnappings in your country."

"Yes, and they're ruthless. They're hell bent on destabilizing us as a nation," Ferrari said, disgusted.

"I read about them. Some college kid started it about ten years ago, right?

"You know all that?" Ferrari pushed out his lower lip and nodded his head. "I'm impressed."

"I read the *Corriere della Sera* when I can get my hands on it. They want to take down the so-called imperialist state of the multinationals, right?" Mickey said.

"Right. And they're bad, really bad. They keep kidnapping and killing politicians and industrialists."

"Man, that's terrible."

"You got that right. The bastards use any means possible to try and subvert our political system and cause chaos. Nothing's beneath them—bank robberies, drugs and arms trafficking, homicide, kidnapping—anything they can think of. It's a huge problem and we've got to stop them before it's too late."

Mickey put his hands on his hips and let out a sigh. "I get it. No wonder no one answered the phone."

Just then, two detectives walked in.

"Detective Gallo, these are Detectives Rossi and Lombardi, the men that have been assigned to your case," Ferrari said as the men shook hands and introduced themselves.

"Glad to see you guys. Can we make a move now? I'll tell you everything on the way into the center of Milan," Mickey said.

"Right, follow me," Rossi said.

He led the way out of the police station, through the pouring rain and over to a waiting car. Mickey intuitively took the backseat behind Lombardi and Rossi. Lombardi turned on the engine and the group took off toward the expressway.

"Damn," Rossi said as he wiped off the condensation that had formed inside the car. "This rain is terrible."

The men wiped the windows with the sleeves of their coats and peered out at the traffic, which had come to a complete standstill. Without hesitation, Lombardi reached over and turned on the blower and the patrol car's single flashing light, deciding to leave the siren off for the time being. Once the condensation lightened up, he revved up the engine and began racing through the emergency lane.

"If it's alright with you two, I'd like to start by first checking in at my niece's residence to see if she is OK," Mickey said, handing Rossi the torn piece of paper containing Anna's address.

"Of course. Let's see where we need to go." Rossi looked at the address.

"It's called La Principessa," Mickey said.

Lombardi and Rossi glanced at each other knowingly because La Principessa was famous in Milan for housing a smattering of the most magnificently beautiful foreign women in the world who had come to model Italian fashions.

"We should be there in about fifteen minutes," Lombardi said.

A few moments later Rossi turned and looked back at Mickey. "So, tell us more, Detective Gallo."

Mickey started from the beginning and told the entire story in minute detail, beginning with Rhonda's gruesome murder. Fortunately, the detectives took every word he said very seriously. He was a fellow Italian after all, and if this is what he said, this is what they believed.

"Why are you convinced that this guy—by the way, I know who you're talking about—is the killer?" Rossi asked.

"You know him?" Lombardi asked Rossi.

"No, I don't know him personally. I mean to say, I've seen his pictures."

"Really? I've never seen them," Lombardi said.

"Yeah, well my wife buys those gossip magazines and he's in it with all these beautiful women."

"Go figure," Lombardi said, turning off the highway and meeting up with a pile of stationary cars. "Oh shit!" Traffic was at a standstill and Lombardi realized that they were going to have a next to impossible time getting through the streets. "Should I put on the siren now so we can try to get through this traffic jam?"

"Go ahead," Rossi said.

As the siren wailed to life, cars and pedestrians scrambled to move out of the way, allowing Lombardi to maneuver the unmarked police car through the maze of streets haphazardly woven together. Forced to drive up onto the sidewalks, startling shopkeepers busy rolling up their metal shutters so they could open again after their long lunch, the team made headway for a while. Eventually the Alfa

Romeo reached a point where the traffic was so thick even they were having tremendous difficulty getting through.

Lombardi, remembering a shortcut, suddenly jerked to the left and turned down a tiny medieval cobblestone street, allowing the unmarked police car to cut through the clog of traffic and make it through to La Principessa. The car screeched to a halt and the men jumped out and headed into the residence, startling the daytime porter seated behind the reception desk.

"You're the porter here, right?" Rossi asked after the men showed the porter their identification.

The porter was speechless; he had never had the lobby swarmed by police officers before.

Mickey pulled out a photo of Anna and placed it under the porter's nose. "Have you seen this woman?"

"Why, is she in trouble?"

"Could you please just answer the question," Rossi said forcefully.

"Yeah, I remember seeing her this morning," the porter said.

"You did? What time?" Mickey asked.

"She left early. I think it was around 7:00 a.m."

"Did she say where she was going?" Mickey continued.

The porter, really confused and wondering why this American woman would bother telling him where she was going, just shook his head no.

"Did she leave alone?" Rossi asked.

"No, actually, some good-looking guy came to pick her up."

Mickey turned pale as a sudden queasiness settled in the pit of his stomach. "What guy?"

"How would I know what guy?" the porter responded. "All I know is that he was tall and muscular, with blonde hair and a beard and mustache."

"Was he Italian?" Lombardi asked.

The porter thought for a second. "No, the two of them were speaking in English."

A wave of relief came over Mickey's face and his stomach relaxed as he realized this guy wasn't Franco Rubelli.

"Has she been back?" Rossi asked.

The porter was totally confused. Why was this redhead so important? "No, I haven't seen her."

"You're sure about that?" Rossi asked.

"Yeah, I'm sure."

"Why don't you buzz her apartment anyway," Mickey said.

"Listen, I've been doing this job for forty years, OK? I even know when the mice come home."

"What?" The confused interrogators looked at each other.

"I'm just saying that no one can get past me when I'm at my desk, which is every day between 6 a.m. and 4 p.m., except Sunday, and she hasn't returned."

"Don't you take lunch?" Mickey asked.

The porter lifted a lunchbox. "My lunch."

"What about going to the bathroom?" Rossi asked.

"It's right here next to the elevator. The door chimes, so I can hear if someone comes in, which they didn't, OK?"

"Just buzz her apartment," Rossi said.

The porter, completely annoyed now, leaned over, and with an exaggerated motion, buzzed Anna's apartment for a full ten seconds. There was no answer.

"You sure that was her apartment?" Rossi asked.

The porter didn't even bother to answer.

"So you're sure she left?" Lombardi asked.

Again, the porter refused to answer. He looked at the men with an irritated smirk.

"OK, OK. We're wasting time here," Mickey said. "Let's head over to this guy Franco Rubelli's agency."

Lombardi suggested they call first to see if Rubelli was there.

"We're not calling anywhere first," Rossi said. "You want to give this creep Rubelli a heads up that we're coming to get him so he can skip town? How about the element of surprise?"

Lombardi dropped his head in shame. He realized it was a stupid question and he should have known better than to suggest it.

"OK, let's make a move." Detective Rossi scribbled a phone number on a piece of paper and handed it to the porter. "If you see the American lady come back in, ask her to call this number."

They thanked the porter and started walking out of the residence, but then Rossi stopped and turned back. "You live here, right?"

"Yep, downstairs," the porter responded, offering no further discussion.

"OK, if we buzz you, no matter what time, make sure to let us in," Rossi said.

"Ya, ya. I'm always home anyway."

The men headed out the door and to the police car. As they got into the car, Mickey handed Lombardi the address to Rubelli Models. Lombardi put on the siren, pressed on the gas and wove through the small clogged arteries called streets, soon reaching the impressive Italianate building housing Franco Rubelli's modeling agency. Rossi was first out of the car and quickly made his way to the huge, solid wood, antique, brown double doors and pressed the buzzer for Rubelli Models on the multi-unit door panel. Mickey and Lombardi soon stood behind Rossi as the group of detectives waited for an answer.

"They might still be closed for lunch," Rossi said, looking down at his watch and noticing it was 4 p.m.

"Buzz again," Mickey said when no one picked up the intercom.

Just then, a tiny homely woman about thirty years old approached the double doors. The detectives moved out of the way and the woman unlocked the doors and stepped into the opulent, plant-filled courtyard. Mickey, realizing that no one was answering the buzzer, decided to ask the woman about the agency before the doors shut behind her.

"Excuse me, miss?"

Franco's assistant, Dawn, turned toward the detectives. "Yes?"

"I'm Detective Gallo and these are Detectives Rossi and Lombardi. We're looking for Franco Rubelli. Do you know him?"

She looked the three detectives up and down, memories of her experience with police officers resurfacing.

"Miss, we asked you a question," Rossi said.

"Yes, I know him. I work for him actually," she said finally.

"You do? What's your name?" Mickey asked.

"Dawn."

"Dawn who?" Rossi asked.

"Dawn White."

"Your name's familiar," Rossi said.

Dawn didn't offer up any information. She didn't like talking about her past. The memories were too painful. Leaving Chicago with her family when she was only three, then moving to Milan for a year before moving back to Chicago, were a blur. Memories of her father being arrested, extradited back to the States, and sent to prison in Illinois, were not. Neither were the memories of visiting him in prison every weekend until he was killed in a fight on the yard. After his death, she and her mother moved back to Milan. The lack of stability took its toll on Dawn. She was emotionally scarred.

"Isn't your father Billy White?" Rossi continued.

"Was." Dawn lowered her eyes in sadness.

"Was? Sorry to hear about that," Rossi said, remembering her father well. He was a big-time drug dealer from Chicago. Pictures of his cute little daughter crying her eyes out were smeared all over the Italian news when he was arrested and extradited. Funny how she didn't change, except she was no longer cute—she just looked like someone with dwarfism.

"OK, Miss White, do you know where your boss is right now?" Rossi asked, trying to get back to the issue at hand.

Dawn didn't respond immediately, silently challenging the detectives. She wanted to divulge as little information as she possibly could. "Why do you need to find him so desperately?" she asked.

"Ma'am, this is police business. Please just answer the question," Lombardi said.

She still didn't answer, causing Rossi to flare up. "Don't obstruct justice. Tell us now!"

"I don't know where he is. He could be anywhere," she replied.

"Well, do you know where he lives?" Mickey asked.

Still holding the heavy wooden door open, she lifted her free hand and pointed up.

"Upstairs," she said, motioning to the large, multi-apartment, U-shaped building surrounding the courtyard.

"Which unit?" Rossi asked.

Once again Dawn took her time answering, her disdain for the detectives obvious. After a long pause, she finally responded. "He has the whole top floor."

"Which one is the buzzer for his residence?" Mickey asked, searching the door panel.

Dawn casually turned toward the door and buzzed a nameless button located at the bottom. The detectives glanced at each other and then over to Dawn. There was still no answer.

"Guess he's not in," Dawn said.

"And you don't know where he is?" Rossi said.

"No, I don't. I'm not his wife," Dawn said emphatically, though she wished desperately that she was, or at least one of his mistresses. She buzzed one more time, sure that he probably was up in his apartment, but most likely occupied with one of his lovers since his girlfriend was on location in the Seychelles modeling bathing suits. Seething, Dawn nevertheless courteously looked at the detectives and then pointed to the darkened windows on the top floor at the back of the courtyard. "I don't think he's home."

The men looked up at the apartment, darkened with heavy closed curtains, and realized she was probably right.

"Go take a look anyway," Rossi said to Lombardi.

Lombardi went into the courtyard and then up the stairs two at a time.

"Where does he like to eat?" Mickey asked, completely exasperated by this woman, whom he instinctively disliked.

Dawn spouted out a few of the restaurants she knew Franco preferred. "Bon Bon, La Magenta, Piccolo Bar, La Strega, Furno, La Bella. That's pretty much it."

Knowing all the restaurants would be closed now, Rossi asked, "What time do you expect him back at the agency?"

"He's not in the agency today. And tonight he has a big dinner and party."

"Party? Where?" Mickey asked.

"I don't know," she lied.

"So what's the party for?" Rossi asked.

"Federico Lama, of course."

"Federico Lama?" Mickey and Rossi looked at each other and then back at Dawn.

"The designer?" Dawn said condescendingly. "Everyone knows his show opened Milan Fashion Week today."

"Right, right. Milan Fashion Week," Rossi said.

"What's Milan Fashion Week?" Mickey asked.

Rossi turned to Mickey. "It's when all of the Italian fashion designers show their new collections."

"I see. I think Anna mentioned something about that."

"It happens a few times a year," Rossi continued. "Thousands of fashion people from around the world descend on this city, causing huge traffic jams and more chaos."

Dawn stood by coolly during the banter between the two detectives until Mickey turned to her and asked where the shows were held. She mentioned a few venues, and Lombardi, who by now had returned, wrote down the info.

"And the dinner tonight?" Mickey asked.

"I have no idea. Probably one of those restaurants I mentioned."

"Aren't you going?" Mickey added.

Mortified, Dawn looked down at the ground and barely uttered the word no.

"What about the party? Do you know where the party is being held?" Rossi asked.

Dawn knew full well it was probably being held at Nepentha nightclub, but she decided not to give the detectives that information. "Look, I really don't know. There are lots of nightclubs in Milan. Could be anywhere." She rattled off a few names, other than the most likely one.

"Alright, you've been a big help. By the way, can you give us your boss's phone number?" Rossi said.

"Certainly." Dawn provided the number without hesitation, knowing that anyone who called Franco had to use his code—ring twice, hang up, then call again—otherwise he wouldn't answer.

While Lombardi scribbled down the number, Rossi reminded Dawn that if any of the information she had given them was incorrect she could be held responsible for obstruction of justice.

Dawn wasn't worried. She'd told the truth. She simply omitted certain details.

"And the model Anna McKenna? She's with this agency, right?" Mickey asked.

Perplexed, Dawn looked to Mickey. "Why?"

Mickey suspected she was doing her very best not to be forthcoming and he was fed up with her. Raising his voice, he asked, "Where is she?"

Caring little about the new American model, who she considered to be a lucky snob with the good fortune of having been born beautiful, she decided to answer truthfully. "She modeled in Federico's fashion show earlier, but it ended around noon."

"Do you know where she is?" Rossi asked.

"How would I know, I'm not her—"

"Babysitter. Right, we got it," Mickey said.

The three men headed back to the police car and radioed the station, asking the policeman who answered to try the phone number Dawn had given them. No answer.

"Damn, we're getting nowhere fast," Rossi said. "Let's go check some of those venues were the shows are being held and see if we can find them there."

Mickey agreed with that plan, but was getting more and more nervous. He was hoping to find Anna and Franco before the sun went down. Before tragedy happened again.

CHAPTER 23

ANOTHER PARTY

O nce the fashion show ended, most of the models scampered off to model in another one scheduled for 4 p.m. in a different part of town. It wasn't the case for Anna, though. As Franco had pointed out, her late arrival in Milan due to her bout with the flu had hindered her possibilities to model in other shows. Also, because the city was alive with fashion fever and anyone who was anyone in the fashion world was occupied with Milan Fashion Week, the rest of the fashion world was on hold, leaving Anna free for the rest of the day. Coincidentally, Paul had the day free as well, and so the two decided to spend the afternoon walking around the streets near Piazza Del Duomo, home not only to Milan's magnificent Gothic Cathedral, but hundreds of clothing boutiques. After spending some time taking in the beauty of the square and the surrounding boutiques, the two happened upon Fiorucci, Milan's hottest boutique of underground fashion.

"Far out," Paul said, peering at Fiorucci's window display filled with male and female mannequins. The mannequins had on an assortment of trendy clothes, all in bright colors, and were surrounded by strobe lights, creating a photography studio setup.

"Hey, let's go in. I want to try on those fuchsia-colored jeans," Anna said.

"Me too," Paul quipped.

"You want try on fuchsia jeans?" Anna said, horrified.

"Nah, I think I'll stick with blue." Paul held the entrance door open and followed Anna into the enormous boutique.

"This will match my jeans," she said, grabbing a fuchsia feathered boa and wrapping it around her neck.

"Not bad," Paul said. He grabbed a white feathered boa and noosed it around his neck, then yanked it and let his head fall to the side while sticking out his tongue, as if he had been strangled. Before Anna could respond, he threw the off the boa. "Hey, look over there." Paul pointed to a corner featuring an outlandish display of female mannequins on roller skates.

"Do you know how to roller skate?" Anna asked.

"Sure, I skate in Central Park all the time."

"Hey, will you take me sometime?"

"Only if you wear this," Paul said, pointing to one of the elaborate mannequins decked out in lime-green spandex leggings, a coordinating fuchsia top, and a gold lamé matador jacket. The wild outfit was topped off with a fuchsia, sequined beany cap, gold lamé elbow pads and gold lamé ankle wings.

"No way." She grabbed Paul's arm and pulled him over to a section filled with brightly colored plastic handbags. "I could use one of these," she said as she peered at the handbags featuring Fiorucci's logo of two cheeky angels in sunglasses, modeled after Raphael's cherubs.

"Can it wait? I'm starving to death," Paul said, his mood changing.

"Yeah, let's go. I don't need fuchsia jeans after all."

The two decided to eat at a popular restaurant in the Galleria Vittorio Emanuele II. Lunch passed quickly and the enamored couple was lingering over their second espresso macchiato—Italian coffee with a touch of milk—and talking about their respective families back home. Anna confided in Paul about her parents' deaths when she was a young girl. She spoke about life growing up with her grandparents and Joey's problems, particularly his eye issues.

"Look, I'm sure everything will work itself out. The fact that you can earn enough money to pay for tutoring and an eye operation is bound to influence his progress."

"Thanks for saying that. It's my biggest hope and really the main reason why I'm here. I want to go back and take New York by storm, as the saying goes."

"No doubt you will."

"Thanks, Paul, I appreciate your confidence in me," she said, smiling as she looked down at her watch and noticed it was already 4 p.m. She really wanted to go back to her residence and rest a bit before the dinner and party later that evening. "What do you think, should we make a move?"

"Sounds good to me," Paul agreed.

"I'll have just enough time to take a little nap before this dinner and party tonight."

"A nap?"

"Yes. I'm really not used to these late nights," Anna lamented.

"Me either, to tell you the truth."

"Also, I'm not used to eating dinner so late. If I sleep a bit, I won't realize how hungry I am."

Anna and Paul both laughed about the late dinners in Italy compared to the usual American dinnertime of 6 p.m.

"You're going tonight, right?" she asked.

"Kind of have to, no? I mean, if you want to work for Rubelli Models you need to be seen in the right places," Paul replied.

"You're right. It's definitely not my thing though. I'd much rather stay in and read."

"I agree, but at least the food is good. Hey, do you want to go together?"

"I'd love to," Anna responded, trying to hide her eagerness.

They paid the bill and then meandered through the quaint streets, reaching Anna's apartment just in time for another onslaught of freezing winter rain. Not wanting to force Paul to walk through the deluge, she invited him up to her apartment and the two talked and listened to some of her favorite Carly Simon songs, drowning out the rather depressing pitter-patter emanating from the continual downpour.

Anna covered her mouth and let out a long yawn. "Excuse me. I guess I'm really exhausted. I think I need to take that little nap I mentioned earlier."

"Of course." Paul stood up, ready to go out the door despite the pouring rain.

"Paul, it's still raining like crazy outside. You don't have an umbrella and neither do I. In fact, I can't believe I still haven't bought one considering how much it rains here."

"Hey, a little rain never hurt anybody."

Anna looked out the window. "You call this a little rain?"

"Well, you have a point."

"Listen, why don't you rest on the couch until it stops, or at least slows down. I'll just go and lie down in my bedroom."

"Are you sure?"

"Absolutely," she said. She walked into her bedroom, closed the door and discreetly locked it.

Forty-five minutes later, Anna woke up to the soft music of her alarm clock and wandered through the living room over to the kitchen for a glass of water, noticing that Paul had never left and was comfortably splayed out on her couch snoring away. She didn't have the heart to wake him up, so just let him snooze while she quietly freshened up and changed into her only fancy outfit—a striking, strapless, black satin jumpsuit.

"Paul, wake up," Anna said, gently shaking him until he slowly opened his eyes. "It's already past seven."

"Oh crap!" he said, quickly sitting up and wiping his eyes. "Wow. You look amazing. You're all ready?"

"All ready to go," Anna said, smiling.

"I think we're gonna be a little late," Paul said.

"Oh well, it is Italy after all. No one will care," Anna said jovially.

"You're right. Hey, why don't you come with me to my apartment so I can shower and change, then we can go to the restaurant from there."

"Good idea."

Anna grabbed her short, black, fake fur coat and a little evening bag and the two dashed out the door and hurried down the street and around the corner.

"Make yourself comfortable," Paul said, motioning to the sofa in his tiny living room while he quickly unbuttoned his shirt, revealing his toned torso, and headed down the hallway toward his bathroom.

Anna sat back, closed her eyes and immediately started daydreaming—about Paul.

Less than ten minutes later, he reappeared looking incredibly debonair in his one and only nice pair of slacks and designer shirt and smelling heavenly of the new musky cologne he'd bought.

"You know what?" Anna said. "I just figured out where I've smelled your cologne before."

"Huh?"

"Remember when I walked into your apartment the first time and smelled it? I thought it was a candle or something and you told me it was the new cologne you had just bought."

"Right, because I wanted to be more sophisticated," Paul said, faking an air of arrogance.

"And that you are," Anna said jokingly. "Anyway, remember I told you I recognized the smell but couldn't place it?"

"Yeah, I remember now. What about it?"

"I just figured it out. It's the same cologne Franco wears," she said, her face scrunching up just thinking about the guy she had grown to loathe.

"No kidding. I didn't even realize that."

"Well, you wear it much better, if I say so myself."

Anna bashfully gave him an approving look while he put on his leather jacket. The two headed out the door and caught a taxi with the hopes of arriving at the restaurant a little after 8 p.m. Fortunately the city had emptied out, making it easy for the taxi driver to weave in and out of the tiny cobblestone streets and squares and eventually stop in front of an obscure little restaurant hidden behind a small patio bordered by attractive potted evergreens.

"This is it," the driver said.

"Thank you," Anna said in Italian while Paul paid the driver.

They headed into the restaurant and were met with an onslaught of commotion emerging from a room filled with boisterously beautiful people—mostly models—seated around a massive table smoking, laughing and drinking wine while doing their best to act the part of sophisticated, special beauties in front of Franco Rubelli. Franco was seated at the head of the table, and the hottest designer in Italy was seated at the other. The animated group barely noticed as Anna and Paul took the remaining two seats.

Paul turned to Anna after their glasses were filled with red wine. "Cheers!"

Anna clicked his glass and promptly put hers back on the table.

"You don't like wine?" he asked after taking a sip.

"How did you guess?"

Animated chitchat continued around the table, and before long Franco called a toast. As he lifted his glass and prepared to drink, he locked onto Anna's eyes, holding his gaze and daring her not to drink.

Why is he looking at me? It made her uncomfortable. Not wanting to antagonize this man, who had the power to make or break her career, she felt she had no choice but to lift her glass and take a sip along with the rest of the group. Three or four toasts later the crowd finally received little pizzas of all persuasions, but by then the wine Anna had felt forced to drink had already gone to her head. Enthusiastic bantering continued while the lively group of elite fashionistas ate, drank and smoked before heading down the dark, deserted streets to Nepentha, one of the hottest nightclubs in Milan.

CHAPTER 24

WASTING TIME

Mickey and his Italian escorts were still unable to find Franco or Anna. They had gone to the venues hosting fashion shows that day and encountered a madhouse of fashion people, but not the two people they were actually looking for.

"Hope your niece is here," Rossi said, turning back to Mickey as the car pulled up to La Principessa.

"So do I. You two can wait here," Mickey said. "No need for all of us to go and check."

He walked over to the entrance of La Principessa. By this time the porter had gone home for the day, so Mickey searched the entry panel and buzzed number 205, Anna's apartment. There was no answer. He buzzed again and peered through the glass doors into the modern lobby. Two tall, stunning, young female models emerged from around the corner of the lobby and headed toward the entry door. Startled, Mickey stopped peering in and backed away, ready to hold the door open while the girls exited.

"Grazie," both girls said to him as they walked through the doorway.

Mickey nodded politely.

"Did you see his green eyes? He's absolutely gorgeous," one said to the other in English.

"Thank you," Mickey responded instinctively.

Not expecting him to speak English, both giggled with embarrassment and quickly ran off, leaving Mickey with entry into the apartment building. He went in and took the stairs up to the second floor and knocked on Anna's door. No answer. *I hope she's not in there.* He began panicking as the two murders resurfaced in his mind. He tried turning the doorknob, but it was locked. He pulled out his only credit card and slid it between the side of the door and doorframe, easily opening it and walking into the apartment. A scent of perfume lingered in the air.

"Anna?"

There was no answer, so he switched on the lights and walked into the tiny kitchen and then over to the bedroom. "That's her coat," he said as he looked down at the forest-green peacoat slung over a bedside chair next to an open closet. Satisfied that it was indeed Anna's apartment, he continued into the bathroom. The sink was still wet. He clenched a section of the hand towel, noticing it was still damp too. She had definitely been there recently. He left the apartment and returned to the waiting police car.

"She's not home," he said to Rossi and Lombardi. He looked at down at his watch. "It's 7:20. I think she was here recently, but left for the evening."

"Maybe she went to the grocery store or something," Lombardi said.

"Possibly, but I don't think so."

"Let's wait here ten more minutes to see if she shows up. The restaurants don't open until 7:30 anyway," Rossi said.

"Yeah, and the stores are about to close, so if she did go shopping she'll be coming home soon," Lombardi added.

"We can wait, but I'm pretty sure she went out for the evening. When I went into her apartment I noticed a strong scent of perfume."

"Maybe she left to go to the dinner that woman Dawn White mentioned." Rossi turned toward Lombardi. "Did you scribble down the restaurants she told us about earlier?"

Lombardi pulled out a piece of paper. He had written all of them down, so he thought. Unfortunately, he had forgotten La Bella, the restaurant where the dinner was being held.

Rossi looked at the paper. "Bon Bon, La Magenta, Piccolo Bar, La Strega, Furno. I haven't been to any of these restaurants. What about you, Lombardi?"

"Are you kidding? On my salary?"

"Well, do you know where these restaurants are?" Mickey asked.

"It's our job to know," Rossi responded. "I say we start by checking out the closest one."

"Good idea," Mickey concurred.

Bon Bon was around the corner, but they took the car anyway and pulled right up to the front window. The men could see a smattering of patrons already seated in the small restaurant behind the sheer white curtains. They walked in and pulled out their identification. All the patrons stopped talking and looked over at the detectives. The maître d', who had been busy taking a couple to their table, spotted the unusual group of men and immediately headed back to the front to see what they wanted.

"Gentlemen, what can I do for you?" he said, trying to hide his nerves. He had recently been in trouble with the law and thought they were there for him.

"Do you recognize this girl?" Mickey said, pulling out a picture of Anna.

The maître d' took the picture and looked at it. He was perplexed and wondering what this girl had to do with him. "No, I don't," he said, handing the picture back to Mickey.

"I see," Mickey said. He put the picture back in his wallet while scouring the restaurant for any sign of Anna or Franco.

"Can you tell us if anybody from the fashion world is here tonight?" Rossi asked.

Relieved their inquiry obviously didn't have anything to do with the car theft he was involved in, he replied jovially, "No models, if that's what you mean."

Rossi and Lombardi looked over to Mickey. The restaurant was small and it looked like the maître d' was right. No one looked even remotely like a model. It was always obvious when models were in tow—they stood out like a sore thumb.

"Where's your bathroom?" Mickey asked. He didn't really need it, but wanted to get a better look inside the restaurant to make sure that Franco Rubelli wasn't in the corner, or even in the bathroom for that matter.

"Straight to the back on the left."

"Give me a minute," Mickey said to Rossi and Lombardi.

He weaved his way through the eclectic crowd of gawking patrons, inconspicuously taking in everything he saw, and then went into the bathroom. Franco wasn't there, so he washed his hands and came out.

"OK, I'm ready," Mickey said. He turned to the maître d'. "If that girl in the photo we showed you comes in, let us know."

"Yeah, right. Call police headquarters immediately and speak to Officer Lordi," Rossi said as he scribbled the phone number on a piece of paper and handed it to the maître d'.

"Of course, of course I will," the maître d' said, now anxious to get them out of the restaurant.

Mickey and the detectives went back to the car and sped off, arriving at the next restaurant fifteen minutes later. This time the maître d' wasn't so friendly. It wasn't going to look good to his customers if detectives were snooping around. Nevertheless, he told them he hadn't seen Anna and once again Mickey did the bathroom trick. Franco wasn't there.

"Shit! Where is this guy?" Mickey said to Rossi and Lombardi as they left the restaurant. His nerves were frayed.

"Look, we still have three more restaurants to check out. He's bound to be in one of them," Rossi said.

Another hour passed as they visited two more restaurants, but they still hadn't had any luck and were now heading to Furno, the only remaining restaurant on the list. The men were silent. Mickey was extremely distressed, and Rossi and Lombardi were thoroughly annoyed, wondering if they were on a wild goose chase. Headquarters put them on the case so they didn't have a choice, and at any rate, the whole mystery surrounding the fashion world was much more amusing than tracking down Red Brigades, the Mafia or petty criminals.

Lombardi turned down a cul-de-sac and headed toward a very discreet restaurant at the end, parking right behind an illegally parked Mercedes limo in front of the restaurant's entrance. Inside, a chauffeur dressed in a uniform and cap was lying back in the reclined driver's seat snoring away. The men were suspicious, thinking it could be Rubelli's car.

"Excuse me," Rossi said, tapping on the window and startling the dozing chauffeur.

The chauffeur's eyes opened wide and he immediately sat up, snapping to attention when he saw three men staring down at him. "What is it?" he asked, cracking open an uncommonly thick window.

Rossi pulled out his badge and pressed it to the chauffeur's window. "You're illegally parked."

"I'll move right away," he said as he started up the engine.

"Who do you drive for?" Lombardi asked.

"Marco Mazzi. Why?"

"Mazzi? The big industrialist?" Rossi asked.

"Yeah. Why does it matter?" The chauffeur looked perplexed. "What's going on?"

"Nothing to worry about, just looking for someone. Go back to sleep," Rossi said as the three detectives walked away from the Mercedes toward the entrance to the restaurant.

"What's with the thick windows?" Mickey asked.

"They're bulletproof," Rossi said.

"Why? What's this guy Mazzi afraid of?"

"Lots of things—kidnapping, robbery, murder. You name it," Rossi said.

"Ah, right. The Red Brigades," Mickey said.

"Yep. Anyone who's anyone is a target in Italy these days," Lombardi added.

"Go figure," Mickey said.

Furno was buzzing and the maître d' was running left and right while the owner, Beppe Bianco, a notorious Italian playboy, was schmoozing with everyone. He glanced over to see who had walked in and whether they were regulars and spotted that they were detectives immediately.

"Excuse me," Bianco said, walking up to the front desk. "Men, what can I do for you? Do you need a table?" It would have been a first, but he was happy to offer them a meal.

"No, no. We just have a few questions," Rossi said.

Not at all amused, because it looked suspicious in front his customers, Bianco asked to be questioned another time.

Mickey wasn't in the mood to be put off. He pulled out the picture of Anna and stuck it in Bianco's face. "Have you seen this girl?"

Bianco took the picture and looked at it closely. "Who is she?"

"She's an American model, but she's working here in Milan at the moment," Mickey said.

"Don't know who she is. Why are you looking for her?"

"We just are. We're also looking for a guy named Franco Rubelli," Rossi said.

Bianco stifled his surprise. Rubelli was a frequent client of Furno, but his restaurant was known to be the most private restaurant in town and he wasn't about to divulge information easily. As for the girl, he had never seen her before and couldn't care less about her privacy.

"One minute." Bianco took the photo and went to the back of the restaurant into a small room. A minute later he came out. "She's not here," he said to the detectives.

"Oh, so she was here?" Mickey asked.

"No, no, I mean no one knows who she is."

"Who did you ask?" Rossi asked

"Also, why did you go back to that room?" Mickey pressed.

Bianco was starting to get angry. Although he didn't like to antagonize officers of the law, this group was badgering him for information he didn't have. "There happens to be a well-known industrialist, who also owns a modeling agency, in the back room eating dinner with some of his girls."

The detectives' curiosity peaked as they looked at each other.

"We'd like to speak with him," Rossi said.

"Oh, I don't think so. He doesn't like to be interrupted," Bianco said, fed up and ready to vigilantly protect the privacy of his clients.

Not taking no for an answer, Rossi, Lombardi and Mickey began heading to the back room without waiting for permission.

"Wait, wait, wait," Bianco said forcefully. "Do you have a warrant? You're upsetting the customers." He knew his clientele was looking on suspiciously. This wasn't good for business and he wanted to prevent these men from snooping.

The detectives stopped in their tracks. They didn't have a warrant and it would take time to get one.

"No, we don't," Lombardi said flatly to the smug Bianco.

"You know guys, I'm hungry. Let's eat something," Rossi said.

"Yeah, me too," Lombardi said.

"Good idea," Mickey added.

Rossi turned back to Bianco. "Give us that table back there."

Bianco, now completely pissed off, knew he had to perform a balancing act between placating the officers and protecting the privacy of his clients. Grudgingly, he grabbed three menus and led them to the only empty table in the restaurant, which just happened to be right next to the adjoining room where Mazzi was holding court with nine beautiful international models.

The three men sat down, making a point of giving Mickey the chair with a bird's-eye view into the adjoining room.

"Guido, come here," Bianco commanded to one of his waiters. "Take care of these men." He walked away, ready to get back to business.

"What can I get for you?" the frazzled waiter asked.

"Minestrone soup and veal Milanese," Rossi said after briefly looking at the menu.

"Same for me," Lombardi said.

"Me too," Mickey added.

"Would you like some wine?" the waiter asked.

Rossi looked at his colleague, then Mickey and back to the waiter. "No, just a bottle of sparkling water."

The waiter scurried off.

Rossi and Lombardi sat looking forward to eating a great meal, one that they certainly wouldn't have to pay for. This was an investigation after all, and either head office would cover it or, more than likely, the restaurant wouldn't charge them. Mickey, on the other hand, was only concerned with finding Anna and Rubelli.

"I need the bathroom," Mickey said. "I'll be right back." He got up, but instead of going to the bathroom, he walked straight into the adjoining room.

"Excuse me," he said to the lively group of beautiful women and Marco Mazzi, who was sitting at the head of the table.

They all stopped talking and looked up at him, allowing him to size them all up quickly. Anna wasn't there, and neither was Franco. Maybe they knew something though. Mickey pulled out Anna's picture.

"Do you know this girl by any chance?" Mickey asked, giving the nearest model the picture. It went around the table and neither Marco nor his concubine of models knew who she was.

"She's not with my agency," Marco said.

"Your agency?" Mickey asked.

"That's right, my agency," Marco replied staunchly.

"That wouldn't be Franco Rubelli Models, would it?"

"What? No way! I would never do business with that piece of shit. He's an asshole!"

"Why is that?" Mickey wanted to know.

"Too long of a story. Anyway, I hate the guy. I never see him."

"So, you don't know where he is?"

"I told you, no," Mazzi said flatly, ending the conversation.

Mickey left the room and got back to the table just as their food arrived. "Rubelli's not in there. Turns out Mazzi hates him, and doesn't think much of his business acumen either," Mickey said to the detectives as they dug into their meal.

"Where is this guy, dammit!" Lombardi said.

"I don't know, but we gotta find the son of a bitch," Mickey said, pushing his food away. He could hardly eat because he was a basket of nerves. Finding Franco Rubelli and Anna was proving to be much harder than he had ever imagined, and his mind kept wandering to gruesome visions of the previous two murders.

"Let's finish up here quickly and search the nightclubs," Rossi said. He turned to Lombardi. "Did you write down the ones that lady mentioned?"

"Right here," Lombardi said, pulling out the list.

Lombardi and Rossi scarfed down their meals in no time and asked for the check, but, as expected, Bianco didn't charge them.

CHAPTER 25

FEELING BAD

"**S**o this is it?" Anna said to Paul as they followed their group into Nepentha nightclub and down the hallway toward the elegant disco room.

"Guess so. It sure is slick, but doesn't compare to Studio 54."

"Still nice though."

"Hey, I need the bathroom. I'll meet you in a sec," Paul said, spotting the men's room. He suggested that Anna, rather than wait for him, go with their group. "I'll find you."

"OK, I'll save you a seat," she said as she turned back toward the lively group.

They made their way into the lounge and to the far side of the room, where a special VIP section with several midnight blue velvet chairs and sofas and dark brown wooden coffee tables were reserved for the privileged coterie. Leading the way, Franco offered the designer and his boyfriend one sofa while taking the one right next to it for himself, making it clear that everyone else needed to sit elsewhere.

He spotted Anna and smiled, looking deep into her eyes. "Sit next to me beautiful," he said, patting the space next to him.

Always aware of everything happening around him, Franco hadn't failed to notice the burgeoning love blossoming between Paul and Anna and was determined to destroy it. All eyes were on Anna while she hesitated, making no move. She had zero interest in sitting next to him, already dismayed by his arrogant and cocky behavior. Besides, she wanted to sit next to Paul. She stood still, unable to move toward him as his eyes turned dark and he continued staring at her.

Just when it started to become a bit embarrassing for the two, a stunning platinum blonde Finnish girl named Pia unabashedly plopped down in the seat next to Franco and immediately started flirting outrageously with him, thwarting the awkward situation. Franco smiled and put an affectionate arm around the provocative young woman, but he was fuming inside. He believed every woman should be in love with him and fixated by the power he generated, and when that didn't happen he reacted poorly.

Paul soon returned and found Anna still standing amongst the large group making claim to the remaining chairs and sofas.

"Hey," he said.

"I'm so glad you're back."

"Are you OK?" he asked as he motioned for Anna to have a seat opposite him at one of the last empty tables, to the side and facing Franco's sofa.

Suddenly the volume went up as one of the latest disco songs started pulsating through the air, signaling the official beginning of the evening's dance music and calling many partiers to the dance floor.

"Well, I was walking with the group—" Anna said.

"What? I can't hear a thing you're saying."

"I was walking into the nightclub while you went to the bath—"

"Can't hear a thing," Paul shouted over the blaring music.

"Never mind," Anna said, motioning through the air to end the conversation.

No sooner had they sat down than the champagne began to flow. *Oh no*, Anna thought, *first wine, now champagne.*

The dance floor was packed, but everyone in Franco's group remained and gave enthusiastic attention as the waiter poured champagne into their glasses. Franco toasted the designer, his boyfriend and all of the models, then turned to Anna and gazed intensely into her eyes while he sipped his champagne, compelling her to drink once again.

Soon the fashion coterie joined the people on the dance floor and began gyrating to the pulsing disco beat. Several songs later, the music slowed down and most of patrons of the nightclub took a seat, leaving a smattering of lovebirds on the floor. Paul took Anna, now rather intoxicated and feeling free as a bird, and pulled her to his powerful chest.

"What's with you and Franco?" he asked.

"What do you mean?"

"Well, why did he stare at you that way when he was toasting the group?"

"He's a control freak and wanted to make sure I drank the champagne I suppose."

"That's strange."

"Well, it probably really boils down to the fact that he wanted me to sit next to him when we arrived and I didn't."

Paul took a minute to think about that. "So you rejected him."

"I guess so."

Aroused by a sense of victory, Paul pulled Anna closer, thrilled that he was the winner in the unspoken competition with Franco for Anna's affections. Anna, equally elated by the sense of protection gleaned by her blossoming love with Paul, enthusiastically returned his embrace. Not having a care in the world, the couple danced sensually together and even shared a long kiss. The song ended and Anna came back to her senses. Suddenly feeling a bit dizzy, she asked Paul to take her over to their group so she could sit down.

"Oh my gosh, another damn toast," Anna said as the group once again lifted their glasses to congratulate someone or something. Anna no longer cared and refused to drink any more. She was definitely feeling the effects of too much alcohol. "Paul, I feel horrible," she said, holding her queasy stomach.

"Oh no, are you going to throw up?"

"I don't think so. Not yet anyway."

"Maybe we should get you back to your apartment."

"Would you mind? I think I've had enough for tonight. I need to go to sleep."

"Of course not, let's get you out of here."

The two politely said goodbye, in particular to the designer, who was now completely intoxicated, and Franco, still very much in control and smiling falsely. His blood was boiling but he hid it well, which was easy to do considering the amount of attention he received from some of the other ambitious models amongst the group.

Paul spotted a taxi waiting nearby and gently helped Anna into the back seat. He closed the door and walked around to the other side, scooting in beside her. Anna gave the taxi driver instructions in Italian and they were on their way. Within seconds she lay her head on Paul's strong chest and fell fast asleep.

CHAPTER 26

LA PRINCIPESSA

"You know, Anna might be back home," Mickey said as he looked at his watch and noticed it was twenty minutes to midnight. "She doesn't like late nights."

"Do you want to stop and check before we scope out the night-clubs?" Rossi asked as the three men got into the car.

"Yeah, definitely," Mickey said.

"OK, Lombardi, let's head back over there first," Rossi said.

Lombardi revved up the engine and sped through the empty streets of Milan, getting to La Principessa in no time at all. The two men waited in the car as Mickey walked over to the entrance and buzzed her apartment several times. There was no answer, so he buzzed the porter's door. A few moments later a groggy, irritated voice came over the intercom.

"Who is it?"

"It's Detective Gallo. I met you this morning."

The porter buzzed the door open without any further questions. Clearly, he was half asleep and couldn't care less. He must get woken up all the time, Mickey thought as he went into the building and raced up the stairs to Anna's apartment. He knocked on Anna's door and waited a few seconds before pulling out his credit card and opening her door. The scent of perfume was gone. He made his way into the bathroom and squeezed the hand towel. It was dry, and so was the sink. She hadn't been back. He closed the door behind him and raced back down to the waiting car.

"No luck?" Rossi asked as Mickey hopped into the back seat.

"Nope." Mickey was more than panicked by now. He was pissed off beyond belief. How in the hell could it be so damn difficult to find two people? Then something occurred to him. What if she was on her way home and they missed her because they were busy looking at the nightclubs. "Maybe one of us should hang out in front of the building and wait for her to return."

"Good idea. Let me radio in. I'll get an officer to come over and keep an eye on this place," Rossi said.

Mickey got out of the squad car to stretch his legs as Rossi radioed in. He found a park bench in the dimly lit square across the street and positioned himself so he wouldn't miss anyone coming in or out. Less than ten minutes later, Officer Esposito drove up and parked his police car behind the unmarked Alfa Romeo. The group chatted briefly about their plan going forward. Mickey pulled out a picture of Anna so Esposito would know whom he was looking for.

So absorbed were they in their planning, no one noticed the taxi that pulled up in front of La Principessa.

"Anna, wake up. We're at your apartment," Paul said.

"Right, right. OK," she said and groggily sat up. "I feel awful."

Paul got out of the car and walked around to her side and opened the door. "Here, let me help you out."

Anna clumsily got out of the car and leaned onto Paul. "I didn't drink that much, did I?"

"No, you didn't. But if you're not used to alcohol it doesn't take much to feel sick," Paul said sadly. Now having any hopes of taking Anna to bed completely deflated, he gently escorted her into the building.

"I'm so sorry I had to take you away from the party," she said, stepping into the lobby.

"Not to worry. I just want you to feel better." He took Anna's elbow and led her into the elevator and pressed the second floor.

"I'm so tired," she said, resting her head on his chest.

The elevator door opened and Paul led her out and down the hall to her apartment and waited while she reached for her keys and opened her door. She turned back to Paul and, smiling weakly, stared into his eyes as she wavered to and fro.

"Look, are you OK? Do you need more help?" Paul said, concerned.

"No, I'm fine. I'm just going to put on my pj's and get into bed." She giggled flirtatiously.

"OK then," he said, unwilling to push for more.

Anna looked into Paul's eyes and thought briefly about asking him to come in, but she was drunk and sick to her stomach. *Not a good idea*, she thought, coming to her senses.

"See you tomorrow?" he asked.

"Absolutely." Anna smiled. "Wait. I have a 10:00 o'clock audition at the agency tomorrow morning."

"I have the same one. I'll pick you up and we can go together."

"Sounds like a plan," Anna said as she saluted Paul and then teetered on her heels.

"OK, bedtime." He kissed her cheek and she grudgingly started closing the door.

"Remember to lock it," he said, and waited until he heard the lock click. Satisfied, he walked back to the elevator, pressed for the lobby, and made his way out of La Principessa.

CHAPTER 27

TIME'S RUNNING OUT

Franco left the dance floor and sat back down on the sofa. He was consumed by an uncontrollable urge for revenge against Anna for snubbing him. He was having a hard time enjoying the party but did his best to hide it, saying the right things, laughing, dancing and toasting all around. But his craving for retribution simmered below the surface and needed to be satiated. He checked the time; it was well past 1 a.m. Sitting back, he crossed his arms behind his head, closed his eyes and hatched his plan. Ever so slowly his anger dissipated and turned to pure excitement. The tantalizing thoughts of what he was going to do to Anna turned him on. He crossed his legs, hiding the obvious. *They're all drunk by now, no one will notice when I leave.*

The Finnish model, Pia, plopped onto the sofa, jarring him away from the vivid visions he was having planning his attack. She was now completely intoxicated. She leaned over and kissed him. He kissed her back, but then his anger resurfaced. *How dare Anna not sit with me this evening! She has no respect for me. No respect for the power I wield. I'll show her, the cockteaser.*

Suddenly, he bit Pia's lip.

"Ouch!" she shrieked. "You bit my lip." She touched her lip and noticed blood. "Look, I'm bleeding."

Franco looked at her lipstick-smeared face. She was, in fact, bleeding. "Sorry about that."

"Oh no, it's dripping on my blouse."

"You better go clean yourself up," Franco said, without the slightest hint of sympathy.

He helped her to her feet and she woozily made her way through the crowd over to the bathroom. He was about to sit back down, but then realized it was the perfect opportunity to leave. He glanced at the crowd still on the dance floor and made his way toward the exit, got his coat and slipped out the door.

ᗃ

"Remember, she has long red hair and is very tall. Sometimes she wears her hair up, and keep in mind she may be wearing a hat, OK?" Mickey said to Esposito.

"Detective, don't worry about this. I got it," Esposito said reassuringly.

Rossi walked back around to his car. "Let's move," he said.

Mickey and Lombardi hoped into the Romeo and the three detectives took off to search the nightclubs, leaving Esposito behind to keep guard at La Principessa. More than an hour passed with no luck. They had one nightclub left on the list, Club Millionaire. The detectives walked in and scoped it out.

"Look at those two girls by the bar," Mickey said. "They look like models to you?"

"You mean the one with the blonde ponytail standing next to the brunette?" Rossi said.

"Yeah, them," Mickey said.

"I think you're right. They're tall, skinny, and besides being dressed in bizarre outfits, they're beautiful," Rossi said.

"Follow me," Mickey said.

The three detectives headed to the bar.

"Excuse me," Mickey said to the two young women.

They turned to him, looking him up and down approvingly.

"Hi there," the brunette said flirtatiously in English.

Not in the mood to flirt under the circumstances, Mickey got right to the point. "I wonder if you could help us?" he asked in English.

"Sure," the brunette said. "What's the matter?"

"We're looking for this girl," Mickey said and pulled out Anna's picture.

"Is she a model?" the blonde asked, her smile fading.

"Yes, an American model working here in Milan."

"Which agency?" the brunette asked.

"Rubelli Models. By the way, we're looking for Franco Rubelli too."

"Sorry to say, we don't know her," the blonde said, looking over to her friend and back to Mickey.

"Yeah, we're not with that agency," the brunette added. "We're with Fabulous Mannequins; much better."

"It is better," the blonde said. "Marco and Gianni are so nice. It's like a family."

"Excuse me, ladies, don't mean to interrupt, but we don't really care which agency is better," Mickey said.

"Right, sorry about that. Anyway, you should try Nepentha," the blonde said. "That's where a lot of the models hang out."

"Nepentha?" Mickey turned to Rossi.

"It's a popular nightclub. That woman, Dawn, didn't mention it so I thought we could pass on it."

"I didn't believe a thing Dawn said, to tell you the truth. I wanna check it out," Mickey said.

The detectives quickly found their way over to Nepentha. Once inside, they could see the place was swarming with models, one more beautiful than another. The detectives looked around as Umberto Tozzi's international hit, "Ti Amo," blared out through the loudspeakers. All the diehard partiers on the dance floor, made up mostly of models, were arm in arm, hanging on to each other and singing along merrily. The detectives headed toward the spirited group, knowing it wasn't going to be easy to break their trancelike state and get information on Anna or Franco.

"Excuse me," Mickey said loudly to a shorthaired female model at the end of the improvised chorus line.

She ignored him, barely noticing he was trying to talk to her. He didn't give up. Eventually she stopped singing and listened to Mickey, but still clung to the raucous group pulling her left and right.

"Do you know this girl?" Mickey asked at the top of his voice as he took out the picture of Anna.

The girl let go of the group and took hold of the picture. "Do I know her? I want to be her," she said drunkenly. "She's so fucking beautiful."

"Yeah, but do you know her?" Rossi asked impatiently.

"Of course I do. It's Anna. Anna Panna," she said sarcastically as her friend, a young American female photographer in Milan hoping to get the opportunity to shoot for some of the elite Italian fashion magazines, came up and joined in the conversation.

"Anna Panna?"

"Yeah, Anna Goody Two-shoes," the model said.

Mickey tilted his head sideways, momentarily perplexed by the nickname they had given Anna.

"Is she here?" Rossi asked.

"No, she left with her boyfriend, Pauly. Pauly Wally," the model said.

The two women could hardly control their laughter.

"It's way past her bedtime," the photographer said, breaking out in hysterics.

Disgusted by their inebriated antics, the detectives continued nonetheless. It was the first break they'd had all night.

"What about Franco Rubelli?" Mickey said, a bit too sternly. "Is he here?"

"Yup," the model said, teetering back and forth. "He's right over there, kissing Pia." She turned and pointed to the sofa where Franco had been sitting moments before. "Oops, looks like he's not there anymore," she said giddily.

"I guess he and Pia left together. Wonder why," the photographer said, voice dripping with innuendo.

"Did anyone see them go?" Rossi asked.

"No," the girls chimed in together.

"Oh, wait," the model said.

"What is it?" Mickey asked.

"Wait, wait, wait! There's Pia. She's coming this way," the model said, stopping Pia as she walked past them.

"Hey, what's wrong with your lip?" the photographer asked, noticing Pia's bottom lip was swollen and deep red.

"Nothing, nothing. Where's Franco?" Pia asked.

"We thought he was with you."

"He was, but I went to the bathroom and now he's disappeared. He must have left," Pia said. She started to cry.

The women paid no more attention to the detectives and started comforting Pia, who was clearly distressed.

Mickey turned to Rossi, panicked and confused and about to blurt out the thought that came to his mind. *What if Rubelli and this guy Paul are in on the murders together?*

"What is it, Gallo?" Rossi asked.

"Never mind," Mickey said, deciding it best not to let Rossi in on his theory. It was too farfetched. "We need to get out of here."

The detectives left the club and hurried back to the car.

"Why don't we drive past Rubelli's apartment building?" Mickey suggested.

"Look, we're not far from La Principessa," Rossi said. "Should we stop there first? See if Esposito has any news?"

"Yeah, let's do that first," Mickey said. "Time's running out."

CHAPTER 28

ONE STEP BEHIND

Franco's mind was racing now. The excitement retreated as anger sucked him back in. *How dare she choose that man Paul over me. How dare she!* Suddenly another thought came to mind as he got into his car and started the engine. *What if he's there? What if he's with her?* He thought about Paul's size. *I can take him. He's big, but I'm sure he's never been in the army.* Franco thought about his army days. He had been known for being unwieldy and brutal, using his anger from a desolate childhood and horrible mother to pummel his opponents, earning him the nickname La Bestia—The Beast.

He took one hand off the wheel and checked the pocket of his trousers, making sure he had the keys to Anna's apartment. He continued planning the crime as he slowly drove toward La Principessa. *If Paul is there, I'll knock him out. That's what I'll do. Then I can do what I want with that bitch.* Franco's mind was boiling over with excitement. He could hardly contain himself, but he purposely started breathing slowly, doing exactly what he told his models to do before a big show. Eventually he calmed down, but his glee dissolved into disappointment when he realized how complicated it would be if Paul was there. S*hit! It would ruin everything. If he's there, I'll have to call it off.*

He spotted a phone booth and jerked over to the side of the road and parked the car. He hopped out and called Dawn.

"Hello?"

"It's Franco."

"Hi Franco, how are you?" Dawn said, thrilled to receive a call from him.

"Put Anna in the booking for Mountain Fashions over in Zurich tomorrow morning. Make sure you get her on the first train out."

"Of course," Dawn said. Her eagerness turned to sadness. Franco hadn't called her to chat, but rather because he needed her to cover for him again. It was always like that.

"I'll take care of it right away," Dawn said. Uncontrollable rage started surfacing. With her free hand, Dawn opened a kitchen drawer and took out the bottle of medicine her psychiatrist had prescribed to keep her emotions under control. She glanced at the bottle and dropped it back into the drawer. No medicine for her, she decided. It would ruin her plan.

Franco hung up without so much as a goodbye and jumped back in the car. He turned off his car lights as he maneuvered down the dark side street leading to La Principessa. *Oh no, a squad car. What the hell?* The squad car's lights were off and the car was empty. Overflowing with adrenaline, he chose to proceed, hoping he'd be in and out before the officer returned. It was two in the morning and everyone was fast asleep, or busy with their lovers. If they weren't and happened to be coming home from a night out, they were most certainly drunk or high and wouldn't even notice him. He continued driving and parked the car on a dark street around the corner and turned off the motor.

ʎ

Dawn was in a trance. She walked over to her closet and opened the door. She took out her black trousers and sweater and slipped them on. Then she put on her black leather jacket and gloves and creeped silently out the door.

ʎ

The piazza housing La Principessa and the surrounding streets were pitch-black. No one could see if someone got out of a car and went to the trunk and opened it. Under the cover of darkness, it would be easy to lift the stiff top layer covered in carpet and discreetly pull out a seven-inch combat knife and black knit ski mask. A dark figure dressed in a black leather jacket, black gloves and black trousers would go unnoticed.

The entrance to La Principessa was dark too. No one would be able to make out a figure putting a key into La Principessa's main entry door. No trace could ever be proven. How many international models were housed in this residence? How many stayed just a month or two at a time? And how many keys had already fallen into the hands of strangers?

ʎ

Officer Esposito, imposing in his black, belted, leather jacket, gray trousers and black beret, paced the dark sidewalk in front of La Principessa. Not only were the streets silent, they were pitch-black due to Italy's new regulation demanding that streetlights be turned off after a certain hour to conserve energy and save money. He had been watching the front door of La Principessa from his squad car for more than a few hours and was dead tired. Bored to death because no one had entered or exited the building the entire time, he finally decided to get out and walk around a bit.

As he hoped, the fresh air began to wake him up, but now he was ready to get back in the car. He heard a loud clatter. Ears perking up, he headed toward the noise. He was certain it had come from behind La Principessa. He pulled out his flashlight and cautiously walked to the back of the building. Three cats were lazily stretched out on a large garbage dumpster. He checked the back entrance to the building and found it was locked. Apart from an overturned metal box near the dumpster, he couldn't spot anything else that could have caused the noise. *Must have been these darn cats.*

⚓

Franco's heart was pounding and a rush of adrenaline overtook him as he crept over to the staircase and slinked up to the second floor. He quietly opened the door leading into the hallway, switched off the hall light for good measure, then walked to Anna's apartment and put his ear to her door. No sound. He tried the door. It was locked, so he reached into his pocket for a copy of the key and slowly unlocked the door. Gingerly, he turned the door handle, opened the door and stepped in.

The apartment was dark apart from a faint light that shined on the living room sofa, highlighting a handbag and black, fake fur coat. He scoured the room for any signs of Paul's clothes, but there were none. *He's not here, otherwise his coat would be somewhere in the living room.* Slowly he crept through the dark hallway toward her bedroom. The bedroom door was ajar, leaving just enough room for him to slyly creep in without a sound. Gently, he put one gloved hand on the center of the door and another on the side of the door, holding it firmly so it wouldn't squeak, and then silently slipped around it.

There she was, alone and lying motionless underneath a white duvet.

What was she wearing? A pink flowered nightgown? How very sweet. Doesn't she look innocent with her soft red hair framing her gentle face. Right. So sweet, so innocent. You can't fool me, you bitch. You know you want me. How dare you pretend otherwise. You're just another cockteaser, like all the rest.

Doing the utmost to control his breathing as his anger consumed him, he slowly crept to her bed.

CHAPTER 29

OBSESSION

*H*ow dare he! *After everything I've done to protect him and hide his sick secret.* Dawn relived the moment Franco had rejected her, when she'd made a fool of herself. She had thought he wanted to kiss her. She'd been ready for the moment, dreamt about it every day. So when they were seated side by side working on an upcoming influx of new models and he leaned toward her, she kissed him. Surprised, he jerked back and looked at her with disdain, making her feel like a fool.

"What the hell are you doing?" he asked. He grabbed the pen he had been reaching for and walked out, leaving Dawn mortified and at a loss for words.

She'd thought she would be fired, sure that he would never forgive her, but later he acted like nothing happened because he knew he couldn't function without her—he really needed her.

Deep down inside he loves me. I know he does. It's those models that cause all the trouble. They taunt and tease him and suck up to him just so they can get work and become famous. If they weren't in the way, he'd realize how much he loves me and how much he needs me. He would be with me, only me. Lucky bitches! I hate every one of them, with their kiss-ass smiles. So innocent. So coy. So... so... fucking BEAUTIFUL!

Though Dawn's mind was clouded with rage, her vision was clear through the eyeholes of her black ski mask. Motionless, she hid inside Anna's closet and peered through a crack in the door. She watched Franco enter Anna's bedroom and slink toward her bed and stare down at the peacefully sleeping beauty.

No makeup and still stunning. Bitch!

Franco gazed down at Anna, her tousled hair framing her near-perfect face. *How angelic.* Sneering, he took off his jacket, laying it on the chair next to Anna's bed. He unbuckled his trousers and slowly got on the bed, careful not to wake his victim. Agile and with utmost precision, he put one of his legs over her hips and straddled her, pinning her down. He curled his lips and leered at her motionless body, still sound asleep. Seething with disdain, he slowly inhaled and spoke. "Cockteaser."

Anna, slightly roused from her sleep, tried to turn over onto her side but was unable to move. Confused, she slowly opened her eyes to see Franco staring down at her. *What?* She blinked several times, unable to comprehend. Franco was smiling, enjoying her startled face as she woke from her slumber.

Terrified, she stared at Franco in disbelief. She panicked and began flailing her arms and straining to get up, but the crushing force of his body straddling her hips and holding her firmly down rendered her immobile. Desperately she tried to escape, but could only lift her back a few inches off the bed.

He looked at her with evil in his eyes, as if a demon had taken him over. Seething with anger, he attempted to thrust himself inside her but Anna moved violently, thrashing about and making it impossible. He was furious. She wasn't going to win. With brute force, he covered her nose and mouth with one of his hands and smashed the back of her head down against her pillow. "You cockteaser! You bitch! How dare you reject me!"

⅄

Still as a statue behind the closet door, Dawn quietly removed her knife from its sheath and pulled out one of Franco's handkerchiefs, holding it to her nose. She sniffed in the scent of his Vanilla Musk cologne and watched as Franco assaulted Anna.

It'll only be a minute or two before he rapes her. Then he'll casually get off the bed as if nothing out of the ordinary happened. He'll remind her that he holds her career in his hands. Remind her that she really wanted him all along, that she asked for it. He'll tell her the police will never believe her—models have a reputation and she's a foreigner in a foreign country—so not to bother. He holds all the power.

Dawn knew the drill so well. How many times had it happened before? Dozens, easily. And he always got away with it. Not one model spoke up or went to the police. It all happened so quickly. Cancel another model from a location booking, one far away of course. *Sorry, she's sick. Why don't you use so and so? She's fantastic.* Before his victim knew it, she'd be in another country. No time to tell anyone. Then she'd either suck it up because of the power he wielded, or leave. Go home or find another agency.

Tears trickled down her cheeks.

Why couldn't he love me instead? I would give him everything he wanted. He wouldn't even have to ask. I would always be there for him.

She began to softly whimper, then stifled her emotions.

He'll see. Once he's behind bars, he'll realize how much he's loved me all along. All those stupid bitches will disappear. I'll be the only one left, the only one he loves.

⅄

Esposito put his flashlight away and headed back to the front of the building, where he noticed the undercover Alfa Romeo parked alongside his squad car.

Rossi rolled down the window as Esposito approached. "Where were you?"

"Behind the building checking out some noise. Turned out to be a bunch of darn cats."

Mickey didn't need to hear more. He jumped out of the car and ran over to the entry panel and buzzed the porter. A few seconds passed before he heard a click and opened the entrance door. Clearly, the porter couldn't have cared less who was at the door and just buzzed it open.

He ran up the stairs two at a time, completely unaware Rossi, Esposito and Lombardi were following him. He reached Anna's apartment and turned the doorknob, which was unlocked. A sickly feeling came over him, draining him of all color as fear embodied him, terrified of what he might find. Despite his apprehension, he forced himself to walk through the darkness toward her bedroom. Rossi, Esposito and Lombardi were close behind. The men could hear something like a mattress squeaking, and a man growling.

"Son of a bitch!" Mickey screamed as he rushed to the open bedroom door.

Moonlight shined through the sheer curtains, revealing a figure dressed in black straddling panic-stricken Anna, pinning her down. Hypnotized by passion and adrenaline, Franco hadn't even realized someone else was in the apartment.

"Stop!" Mickey shouted, switching on the light.

Franco turned toward Mickey, his piercing eyes consumed with anger and lust, and froze. Anna, completely immobilized by Franco's outstretched hand smashing her face and the bulk of his body pinning her to the bed, could only turn her huge, terrified eyes toward Mickey.

"Let go of her!" Mickey shouted.

"Get off the bed and put your hands up," came a voice from behind.

Mickey turned to see Rossi pointing an M51 Beretta pistol at Franco.

Time stood still.

Slowly, very slowly, Franco raised both hands above his head and maneuvered himself off the bed.

Mickey, Esposito and Rossi were at Franco's side instantly, holding him forcefully as Lombardi cuffed Franco's hands behind his back. The Italian lawmen escorted Rubelli out of the building and into the squad car.

⅄

Anna sat on the bed shaking and trembling. Mickey turned off the bedroom light to soften the harsh reality of what had just happened and came and sat by her side. Gently he reached out and put his arms around her and brought her to his chest, slowly rocking her in his arms. He closed his eyes and began singing her favorite childhood nursery rhyme, trying to quell her living nightmare as she sobbed until she had no more tears left.

Neither noticed Dawn creep silently out of the closet, through the darkened bedroom and out the door of Anna's apartment. No one noticed a petite figure in a black leather jacket, black trousers and black ski mask slip out of the front door of La Principessa and into the dark Milan night.

After a while, Anna spoke. "I think it's time I get out of the modeling business."

"Music to my ears, sweetheart, music to my ears."

EPILOGUE

New York

The international news media was abuzz with reports about the capture of the serial killer who'd been freely mingling center stage in the multi-million dollar fashion industry. Though Franco vehemently denied murdering Rhonda or Petra, and the police never found a knife, the story was too good for the press not to run with it.

Franco was extradited to the United States and swiftly convicted of the two murders. The handkerchief holding his Vanilla Musk cologne, along with his fingerprints, sealed his fate. He was sentenced to life without parole and sent to Ossining Correctional Facility (formerly known as Sing Sing), to serve out his life sentence.

Dawn moved to New York City to be by Franco's side, landing a job as a booker at a new, up-and-coming agency. Even though she still hated fashion models, it no longer mattered because now she had Franco all to herself. Every Saturday she woke up early, put together a care package filled with prosciutto, Italian cheese and fruit, and toiletries—in particular, his beloved Vanilla Musk—and caught a train to the prison. It was the highlight of her life.

Anna, too, made headlines when she returned to New York City, and found herself continually bombarded by the media. Too much to handle, she escaped back to her grandparents' home in the country and hid out until the media's obsession with her gradually faded. Although depressed and unable to find new footing, she remained committed to her decision not to continue her modeling career.

That was, until Gianni and Jenny Gavazzi relentlessly began trying to hire her to model for a major designer's entire autumn collection. She finally agreed to make a brief foray back into the world of fashion that originally so intrigued her, then left her completely disillusioned. Despite the queasiness in the pit of her stomach, it was hard to refuse the money she would earn for ten days of work modeling. The fact was, as a model she could earn in a day what took most people a month.

Money isn't everything, she told herself. I will model for this catalogue only and then I will find something else to do with my life. Still, she couldn't quite quash the little voice popping up in the back of her mind.

No you won't, Anna. This is your destiny.

Acknowledgements

I've always wanted to write this book but possibly never would have had it not been for my parents, who raised me to have the confidence to pursue all my dreams, and the help and encouragement from many friends and family members throughout the world. I learned a long time ago that one can rarely achieve anything without significant contribution from others, so I'd like to take a moment and thank the following people from the bottom of my heart.

My editor, Elizabeth A. White, has been instrumental. Without her flawless input, I would have written, quite simply, a scribble of words. I owe enormous gratitude to my husband, Michele, who has spent countless hours listening to me, advising me, and, very importantly, leaving me alone to write in peace. Our daughter, Isabella, has been a terrific source of encouragement, and has kept me accountable and on track. Thanks to my sister Barbara's encouragement and meticulous review, I managed to get past my first draft with a good story in mind.

I owe enormous gratitude to the author of many comedic murder mysteries, Donna Drejza, whom I fortuitously met while dining out. Her ongoing encouragement, enthusiasm, and input have been essential. My dear friend Susan Berger, a mystery lover herself, reviewed my book with meticulous dedication and helped greatly in expanding my story. My good friend Candia Camaggi, a native of Italy, encouraged me and reviewed my story, as did another good Italian friend of mine, journalist Annamaria Waldmueller. Both took the time to review my book and help me spin a story of intrigue and suspense. Finally, my dear, longtime friend Jacqueline Rivers Dunphy, who knows both me and the fashion business inside out, veraciously reviewed my book. With great enthusiasm, she helped me put the whole shebang together!

I'd also like to thank Emanuele Di Stefano, Joe Gorman and Antonio Di Grazia for providing details that help make my fiction read more like a true story.

About the Author

Born and educated in the United States, E. J. Moran began a career as an international fashion model at the age of eighteen when she was scouted by a top modeling agency based in Milan, Italy.

Moran's move to Italy set in motion the rest of her career. She signed with top agents and modeled for famous fashion designers and photographers. Her work took her from Milan to Tokyo, New York, and Paris.

After marrying and starting a family, she retired and continued life as an expatriate in the United Kingdom, Switzerland, Singapore, and Italy, where she divided her free time between teaching English and volunteering for multiple international organizations.

Recently, she put pen to paper to make fictional use of the plethora of experiences she gained during her globetrotting life. Moran and her husband currently divide their time between Europe and the United States.

To be notified of new books and author events by E. J. Moran, sign up at www.ejmoranauthor.com.

Made in the USA
Las Vegas, NV
14 November 2020